NINA LANE

SNOW QUEEN

PUBLISHING

If We Leap
A What If Prequel

Published by Snow Queen Publishing

This book is a work of fiction. All names, characters, locations, and incidents are products of the author's imagination, or have been used fictitiously. Any resemblance to actual persons living or dead, locales, or events is entirely coincidental.

Cover photography: Sara Eirew
Cover design: Concierge Literary Designs & Photography

ISBN: 978-1-7360527-0-9

IF WE LEAP
A What If Prequel
Nina Lane

I believe in us hard enough to take the chance.
But will Cole take the leap of faith with me?

This novella prequel takes place before IF WE FALL.

Reading Order:

IF WE LEAP
IF WE FALL
IF WE FLY

CHAPTER 1

Josie

The Ferris wheel at the end of the Water's Edge Pier spun against the night sky, the lights glittering like multicolored stars. The smells of fried dough and cotton candy drifted on the ocean air along with a cacophony of music. Souvenir shops displayed T-shirts, mugs, and lighthouse knick-knacks plastered with the *Castille, Maine* logo.

Many students from my former high-school strolled among the sunburned crowd of tourists and locals. Growing up in Castille, we'd all spent a lot of time at the pier, from getting ice cream with our families to hanging out with teenaged friends. Though I'd stayed in Castille after graduation to attend the local Ford's College, I'd been so busy with classes and work I hadn't been to the pier at all over the past year.

I was happy to be back after our freshman year, reunited with old friends who'd gone away to college and indulging in the excited nostalgia of our favorite hangout.

"You need to get closer." I plucked a red Lifesaver out of the roll, eyeing my friend Lucy's position at the balloon-popping game booth. "Lean in."

She edged closer to the counter, narrowing her eyes at the fat balloons pinned to the board. She tossed the dart, missing a balloon by an inch. The rest of us—me and our other friends Harper and Emma—groaned in support. I popped the Lifesaver into my mouth and handed the roll to Harper.

She frowned at the top green candy. "You took the red, didn't you? How many did you take out to get to it?"

"Just one." I pushed the candy against my cheek with my tongue. "Don't worry, my hands are clean."

I held up both hands to show her my paint-streaked fingers. She gave me a good-natured eyeroll and took the green Lifesaver. Lucy flung two more darts at the balloon board, popping one. We clapped and cheered. She chose a pink, sparkly plastic bracelet as her prize and fastened it to her wrist.

"Let's try another." She started toward another game booth, then stopped suddenly. "Hold up. Is that Richard Peterson?"

She squeezed my arm and gestured to the tall, blond-haired young man sauntering his way along the pier, two equally good-looking friends at his sides. The radiant light of *college senior, football player,* and *big man on campus,* surrounded him like an aura.

"Big deal," I muttered.

Lucy squeezed my arm harder. "Oh, come *on.* An artist like you should be salivating over his beauty. He was the hottest guy in high school."

"That didn't make him nice." Remembered humiliation stabbed through me. "He and that other guy Peter tried to steal my Halloween candy when I was nine."

"Oh my *God.*" Lucy rolled her eyes. "Hold a grudge much? I gave you a bloody nose when we were seven, and you still became my bestie."

"That was an accident. You didn't know I was behind you when we were climbing the rope ladder."

"My point is that you can't be mad at Richard for something he did ten years ago. They're coming over here. Quick, do I have anything on my face?"

"Just beauty," I assured her.

"Hey." The boys stopped, shoulders slouched, acknowledging us all with casual nods.

"Hey." Lucy's smile widened.

Richard looked at me. "Hey, Josie."

I nodded my *hey* and didn't smile at all.

"How's your sister?" he asked.

Beside me, Harper *tsked*. I could almost feel the wind go out of my friends' sails at the mention of my older sister. Four years older than my own nineteen, Vanessa had been a legend at Castille High, a willowy blond beauty, valedictorian, and track star. Though she'd graduated from college last year, her legendary status lingered.

"She's great," I told Richard. "She's working for an interior design firm. Her boyfriend is getting his MBA at Harvard."

As if you could compete.

He blinked. "That's great."

Emma, who was chatting up Richard's friends Peter and Dave, turned to him. "Hey, you guys want to eat with us? We're heading to McGinty's, then we thought we'd go on a few rides for old times' sake."

"Yeah, definitely. It'll be great to catch up."

Though I wasn't thrilled about breaking bread with Richard and his buddies, I'd make an effort to be friendly. We walked to McGinty's Pub and sat outside at a weathered picnic table near the game booths and arcade.

A server came out to take our orders of fried clams and onion rings, with beers for the men and sodas for us girls. She came back shortly with the drinks, depositing them on the table with a cheery, "Here you go."

"If you want mine, I'll order another." Richard nudged his beer toward Lucy, his eyebrows lifted. "No one will know."

She shrugged and took a sip. He glanced at me. "Josie?"

"No, thanks."

"So, what've you been up to?" he asked. "You're going to Ford's, right?"

"Yes. Majoring in Art."

"That's right." Peter snapped his fingers, as if he'd just made a discovery. "You were super into drawing and stuff, right? You won all the school art shows."

"Her mom teaches art at Ford's," Harper explained. "She has great genes."

"I noticed." Richard kept his gaze on me.

I glanced toward the restaurant. "Oh, look, here comes our food."

We turned our attention to the crispy clams and greasy onion rings. The conversation shifted to stories about college and professors, which soon had us all either laughing or commiserating.

"Isn't that Cole Danforth?" Emma chewed on an onion ring and nodded to the row of game booths. A tall young man, wearing the blue apron of a carnival game operator, stood behind the counter of the Milk Bottle Toss.

My pulse jumped, sparking sudden excitement through my veins. I hadn't seen Cole since last summer. And *oh yes*, that was definitely him—all six-feet-plus, broad-shouldered, thick-hair-the-color-of-chestnuts, strikingly gorgeous Cole Danforth. A thousand little lights flared inside me, illuminating all the secret wishes in my heart.

"Hah." Richard twisted his mouth sardonically and reached for his beer. "Not surprised that douchebag ended up running a game booth."

"He's so weird," Lucy agreed.

"He is not." I was unable to keep the hard note out of my voice.

Lucy raised her eyebrows. "Do you *know* him?"

"Sort of. I mean, not really." Heat crept up my face. I'd known him for eleven years, but I'd always wanted to know him *better*. Trying to conceal my blush, I dunked an onion ring into a puddle of ketchup. "We crossed paths a few times when we were kids. He was always nice to me. It's not cool for you to call him a douche and a weirdo."

Back in high school and even earlier, I'd been deeply stung when someone, especially my friends, disparaged Cole Danforth. Three years older than us, he'd been one of the quieter kids, but ever since I first encountered him in the woods when I was eight years old, I'd been fascinated by him. He'd moved to Castille with his parents when he was eleven, and while his father was the prominent owner of a popular brewing company, Cole had had a reputation for being...well, strange.

"I heard his mom was the weird one." With her forefinger, Harper made a circular motion beside her head. "Like, crazy weird."

"Didn't she commit suicide?" Dave asked.

My insides clenched. We'd all heard the horrible rumors, which had only intensified my empathy toward Cole.

"Yeah, she died when Cole was a senior," Harper said. "She, like, had some sort of breakdown, and Cole's dad had to go to court because she refused to accept help. A judge had to force her into an institution over in Fernsdown. It's kind of sad, actually."

Since Harper's mother worked for the local court, I wasn't surprised by her insider knowledge. I glanced surreptitiously at Cole again. He was taller and bigger than I remembered, and the sun had baked golden streaks into his overlong dark brown hair. Even from a distance, his thick-lashed blue eyes softened the strong angularity of his features, which always seemed to be set in an expression of guarded impenetrability.

"Why's he working at the pier?" Emma asked. "I thought he worked at his father's brewpub."

"Maybe he needs extra cash." Harper took a sip of her soda. "I remember once in high school he had to work at the pier picking up litter. He'd been caught vandalizing a construction site where his dad was building a new pub and brewery, and the judge made him do community service."

"Total douche." Peter reached over to steal one of Emma's onion rings.

"Is he going to college?" Lucy asked.

"I heard he's at Ford's." Richard downed the last of his beer and signaled for another. "Wouldn't be surprised if he dropped out and became a full-time carnie, though."

"I'm surprised he didn't blow up Castille High." Peter snorted with suppressed laughter.

"*Stop it.*" Anger flooded my chest. "You can't keep spreading rumors like that. He got a bad enough rap in high school. Leave him alone in college, for God's sake."

"Whoa." Peter held up his hands. "Didn't know you have a thing for him, Josie."

"I don't," I replied crossly, even though my heart constricted. "I told you—he was always nice to me. You're just pissed that he ran you and Richard off when you tried to steal my Halloween candy."

Both men stared at me blankly for a second before Richard let out a laugh.

"I totally forgot about that." He slapped a hand on his forehead, his eyes dancing with amusement. "We were a couple of little dicks, huh? Too cool for trick-or-treating, but we still wanted candy. Man, Josie, I'm so sorry."

"Josie can hold a grudge like nobody's business," Lucy said. "She's like an elephant."

Richard skimmed his gaze over me. "She doesn't look anything like an elephant."

Lucy kicked me gently under the table—an *omigod, girl!* kick. I shot her a mild glower.

"Water under the bridge," I told Richard dismissively.

In truth, it wasn't him or his bullying that had kept that long-ago Halloween night at the forefront of my memory. The incident had both cemented my belief that people had Cole Danforth all wrong and planted the seed of my crush on him. I'd never divulged my crush to anyone, not even my best friends.

I slid my gaze back to Cole. He was taking a ticket from a customer. His hair flopped over his forehead, and his profile was strong and rigid like the edge of a cliff. He handed three baseballs to the customer and stepped aside.

Then he glanced in my direction. His gaze collided with mine. A shot of energy arced through the air.

Butterflies swirled through my belly. I gave him a subtle little wave. He responded with a tilt of his chin before turning his attention back to his work.

"Cole Danforth is kind of like one of your wounded animals." Harper nudged me in the side. "Maybe you should *rescue* him."

"He doesn't need rescuing." Though my statement was flat, it wasn't lost on me that I'd first encountered Cole in the woods, which was also where I found most of the animals I rescued.

"Can we stop wasting our breath on that loser?" Richard finished his beer and plunked the empty mug back on the table. "Let's go on the rides. Just hold on to me if you get scared, girls."

Harper and I rolled our eyes at each other. We collected our things and started toward the rides. As we passed the Milk Bottle Toss, I couldn't help glancing in Cole's direction again.

My pulse sped up. He was watching me, his gaze hooded and his mouth set in a straight line. I wanted to stop and talk to him, at least to say hello, but I didn't dare give Richard or my friends more ammunition against either me or him.

Reluctantly, I looked away and followed the group toward the carnival.

"Maybe we should have saved dinner until after the rides." Lucy took a few tickets from her purse. "Let's go on the Ferris wheel first so we don't throw up. We'll do the faster stuff later."

"I'll wait here." I stopped outside the railing.

"Come on, Josie, you still can't handle the Ferris wheel?" Harper asked.

That's a big fat nope.

"You go on ahead." I waved them toward the line of people snaking toward the Ferris wheel entrance. "Text me when you're done."

"I'll stay with Josie." Richard planted his arm around my shoulders and hugged me to his side. "Make up for being an ass when we were kids."

Lucy gave me another sidelong *omigod* glance. I eased out from under Richard's heavy arm.

"You really should go with them," I said, as our friends headed toward the line.

"I really would rather stay with you." He winked at me.

Suppressing a groan, I told myself there were worse things in the world than spending a half hour or so with Richard Peterson. We wandered around the carnival, pausing to watch a few people play the strength game.

"Hey, I'll win you something." Richard handed a ticket to the operator of the balloon popping booth. "What do you want, Jo?"

"It's *Josie.* Nothing, thanks."

"Come on, don't you think I can do it?" He waggled his eyebrows encouragingly.

"Okay." I peered at the array of prizes hanging in the booth. My twelve-year-old brother Teddy still liked water guns, so I pointed to a package of two. "How about the water guns?"

"Two water guns coming up." Richard took the three darts. He fired them off without pause, hitting three balloons dead center.

"We have a winner!" yelled the game operator.

"Here you go." Richard presented me with the water guns. "What else shall I win for you? Let's try another one."

His gaze landed on the Milk Bottle Toss booth. He strode toward it.

I hurried after him. "Er, how about the Fishbowl game?"

"I'm an awesome pitcher."

Cole watched us approach, his features hardening. I wished I could let him know I wasn't *with* Richard, but I wasn't sure Cole would even care.

"Give me two games." Richard plunked two tickets on the counter.

Anxiety clutched my insides. I flashed Cole a weak smile. "Hey."

He slanted those thick-lashed, bright blue eyes with little flecks of gold at me. "Hey."

God. One word in his deep voice, and my skin prickled with heat. How would I react if he actually said my name?

"What do you want me to win, Jo?" Richard gestured to the prizes dangling from the booth—stuffed animals, rubber balls, plastic inflatable toys. "Something for you, not your little brother."

I pointed to a large, stuffed black bird with comically big eyes. "That one."

Cole picked up a pole with a hook at the end and detached the bird from the wall.

"Really?" Richard shook his head and laughed. "What about a panda or teddy bear? Why do you want a stuffed crow?"

"It's a raven." I indicated the bird's fuzzy plush beak. "You can tell by the bigger beak and shaggy throat feathers."

"Whatever. I'll win it for you." Richard extended his hand to Cole, who put three baseballs on the counter.

"Knock down all three bottles, and you win the raven for the lady."

"I know how to play." Richard took his time warming up and lining up the ball with the milk bottles.

My body tensed. I wanted to talk to Cole but I didn't know what to say. He'd always had such an air of tragic mystery, like he'd emerged from some gothic novel. Maybe Harper was right that I was attracted to him because he was *wounded*, but aside from being incredibly good-looking, he really had always been nice to me.

For most of my childhood, he'd hovered on the sidelines—along the paths cutting through the woods, in the school corridors, at the harbor, on the pier. Not only had he rescued me from Richard and Peter, more than once he'd brought me something I'd left in the woods—a notebook, my sketch pad, once even Wally, my stuffed rabbit. I'd discovered the lost-and-found items on our front porch the following day and knew they were from Cole. The next time I saw him, he'd always ducked his head and shrugged off my gratitude.

"How long have you been working here?" I finally asked.

"Just for the summer."

"Are you still going to Ford's?"

He nodded.

"Me too. I'm majoring in Art."

"I know. I'm in Marine Sciences."

"You're majoring in Marine Sciences?" I raised my voice to make sure Richard overheard. "Wow, that's really impressive."

It also explained why I hadn't seen him—he likely spent most of his time in the sciences building clear across campus.

Richard's jaw tightened. He threw his first pitch. The ball knocked over the top milk bottle. Groans of commiseration rose from the small crowd that had gathered. Cole folded his arms. Richard pitched the second two balls, knocking over one more bottle but missing the third.

He held out his hand. "I paid for two games."

Cole restacked the milk bottles and put three more baseballs on the counter. Richard pitched them in fast succession, knocking over one bottle this time. Cole cleared his throat. Richard shot him a glare and slapped another ticket on the counter.

"Richard, it's not that big a deal," I muttered.

"I'm winning the damned bird." He pitched again. "I just need to figure out the right strategy."

Cole glanced at me. His eyes crinkled with faint amusement. It occurred to me that I had never seen him actually smile. I smiled back, my belly tensing with nervous anticipation.

Richard paid for two more games and made several valiant attempts before I decided I had to put a stop to this or risk him losing a year's worth of college tuition.

"Hey, we should get back to the Ferris wheel," I said. "They're probably done by now."

Frustration hardened his mouth, but he stepped away from the booth. "Stupid games are rigged anyway."

Spine stiff, he strode toward the rides.

"Do you want a bag for these?" Cole nodded to the water guns I'd set on the counter.

"Sure."

He put the package into a plastic bag and handed it to me. Our fingers brushed, sending a tingle clear up my arm.

"Thanks." I hesitated, wondering how he'd react if I asked him out for coffee sometime. We were longtime acquaintances, so it wasn't like the invitation would be coming out of nowhere.

Richard stopped, his hands spread impatiently. "Josie, hurry it up."

Cole's expression darkened. I gave him an apologetic shrug and grabbed the bag.

"Have a good night." He turned to another customer.

Disappointment rose to my chest as I rejoined Richard. He was checking his phone, his eyebrows pulled together. "They just got on. Damned Ferris wheel takes forever." Letting out a breath, he shoved his phone back in his pocket. "Let's go to the arcade."

Glad to have something to do that didn't involve too much interaction with him, I headed toward the noisy arcade. Machines pinged and buzzed, lights flashed, and teenaged boys alternately cheered and groaned. We purchased several tokens and started playing.

I picked one of the classic *Asteroids* games, setting the plastic bag on the ground to focus on the space battle. I got through two battles before Richard appeared right behind me.

"You do pretty good for a girl," he remarked.

I threw him a derisive look over my shoulder. "You could do better for a guy."

"Hey." He pulled his mouth into a mock frown. "Fighting words."

I turned back to the game, firing at a storm of asteroids and flying saucers spilling from the dark sky. Then Richard put his hand on my ass.

"Don't touch me." I slapped his hand off and tried to move away, but he planted his hands on either side of me and blocked my exit.

"Come on, Josie." He put his head so close to mine his breath brushed against my ear. "You were the only girl in high school who ignored me. But I knew you were hot under your baggy overalls and paint. And you can't tell me you weren't interested."

"I wasn't then, and I'm not now." I shoved my elbow back into his ribs. He grunted but didn't move. "Richard, get the fuck away from me."

"I'm only in town for another week. Why don't we have some fun together?"

"No."

He pushed his pelvis against my ass. Alarm bolted through me, fueling my strength. I shoved him harder, breaking his hold.

As I stumbled away from him, another male figure stepped in

front of me. I looked up at Cole Danforth, his features hard as stone, his cold gaze leveled on Richard. Relief filled me.

"You okay?" he asked me.

"Yes. Richard was just being a jerk." I attempted a smile. "Not that that's anything unusual."

Cole took hold of my arm and moved fully in front of me. Peering around his shoulder, I saw Richard approaching. An angry scowl contorted his face.

"Danforth, you douchebag. Get the fuck away from her."

Cole shook his head, his hands fisting. "You're a bigger asshole than I thought if you didn't understand what she said."

"She's *my* date," Richard snapped.

"I'm not your *date*." Irritation tensed every muscle in my body. "I was putting up with you for my friends' sake, but it turns out you're exactly the scumbag I thought you were when I was nine. You haven't changed a bit."

Richard's mouth twisted into a sneer. "Fucking losers, both of you. Stay the fuck out of my sight."

He turned and stalked away, shoving through the crowd. The tension eased from Cole's shoulders.

"Thanks," I said. "I was only hanging out with him while waiting for my friends."

He bent to pick up the bag I'd left by the game. "Come on, I'll walk you out."

I tucked the water guns into my backpack. As we went back outside to the pier, a fresh wave of anticipation eased my anger. I was alone with Cole Danforth. The movement of his body beside mine, his height and the breadth of his shoulders, inspired a feeling of safety and protection.

And lust. My body had rejected Richard with the speed of a whip-strike, but with Cole...everything tingled and pulsed. If he touched me again, I would light up like a twinkling Christmas tree.

"You seem to rescue me a lot." I shot him a look of wry

amusement. "Especially from Richard Peterson. You're like my hero."

A humorless laugh broke from his chest. "I'm no hero."

"You are to me."

Our eyes met with a sudden charge that arced right into me, electrifying me down to my toes. He broke his gaze first, shoving his hands into his pockets.

"Where are your friends?" he asked.

"They went on the Ferris wheel." I took out my phone and sent Lucy a quick text: *Richard is an ass. Stay away from him. Text me when you're done.*

"Why didn't you go with them?"

"I'm not a fan of heights." I slipped the phone back into my mini-backpack. "Fear of falling, I guess."

A smile tugged at his mouth. "What if you fly?"

I chuckled. "Then I'd be a bird."

"Is that why you wanted the raven?" He tilted his head toward the Milk Bottle Toss booth.

"Yeah. It's kind of silly, but ravens are my favorite bird."

"Why?"

"They have a really cool mythology and history, and they're incredibly intelligent. They also have a strong social structure and mate for life. I just think they're interesting."

Like I think you're interesting.

Cole stopped at the railing overlooking the harbor, resting his elbows on the salt-encrusted wood. I dug into my backpack for a roll of Lifesavers and unpeeled the wrapping. The top one was yellow, and I plucked it out. Beneath was a red one. I popped the pineapple candy into my mouth and extended the roll.

"Want one?"

He looked at the roll. "Aren't the red ones your favorite?"

I blinked. "How did you know?"

"You told me." He shrugged, returning his attention to the harbor. "I saw you walking to school one day when you were...I don't know. Twelve, maybe. A roll of Lifesavers fell out of your backpack. I picked it up and ran to catch up with you to give it back. You gave me a whole speech about how the red ones are cherry-flavored, and cherries were your favorite fruit and cherry blossoms your favorite flower. So every time you had a choice with candy or suckers or Chapstick, you picked cherry. Then you offered me the cherry Lifesaver as a thank you."

A warm glow, like the sun spreading over the cove, filled my veins. "I can't believe you remember that."

"I remember a lot of things about you."

We looked at each other again, and this time the multicolored carnival lights reflected in his irises. Like he had Ferris wheels spinning in his eyes. My heartbeat ratcheted up. As a kid, I'd been fascinated by him, but almost as if he were a movie star or an exotic animal. I could admire him while assuming he would never be interested in me.

Maybe I'd been wrong. I *hoped* I'd been wrong.

"What else do you remember about me?" My voice came out a bit breathless.

"Josie Mays." He ticked items off on his long fingers. "You were a painter of animals. Rescuer of birds. Daughter of an artist and a historian-slash-mailman—"

"Postal carrier," I corrected.

"Postal carrier. Owner of a bright red backpack with yellow daisies. Climber of trees. Favorite of teachers. Occasionally in need of rescuing."

"That about sums me up."

"I know."

"Cole Danforth." I ticked the items off on my fingers. "Explorer of the woods. Worker at the pier. Lover of maps. Secret hero of Josie Mays."

I decided to leave out *target of unfortunate gossip*.

His eyes crinkled with faint amusement. "That about sums me up."

"What am I missing?"

A cloud darkened his expression for an instant. "Swimmer of oceans and lakes."

"You still swim?"

"Whenever I can."

"Where? I never see you at the beach, and I know you're not on the college swim team because my friend Harper's boyfriend is the captain."

"There's a section of Eagle Canyon that's hard to reach," he said. "I found it back when I was a kid. I was running away from home. When it got too dark to walk, I spent the night in these old stone ruins. The next morning, I climbed a rocky slope and discovered an inlet where I could swim and be alone."

My heart constricted. "Why were you running away from home?"

Before he could respond, my phone buzzed with a text from Lucy.

"My friends are done with the Ferris wheel, and they ditched the guys." I slipped my phone back into my bag, disappointed at the thought of leaving him. "I should go back and meet up with them."

He nodded. I wanted to believe a responding disappointment flared in his expression, but he'd always been a tough one to read.

I plucked the red Lifesaver from the roll and held it out in invitation. "Thanks again."

He took the candy and slid it into his mouth, drawing my attention to the movement of his lips. A dusting of stubble coated his strong jaw. I wanted to rub my fingers against it, to see if it felt as sandpapery and delicious as it looked.

Longing gripped my chest. Aside from a couple of short-lived boyfriends, I hadn't yet garnered a lot of experience with men. I'd certainly never experienced the same litany of *feelings* for another man as I had for Cole Danforth over the years.

I stepped back, hitching my backpack over my shoulder. "I guess I'll see you around."

"Yeah." He pushed away from the railing, his gaze on me. "Be careful out there, Josie."

The sound of my name coming from his mouth, as if he were rolling it over his tongue like the cherry candy, elicited a low pulsing in my core.

Turning, I started to walk away. My desire intensified, darkening to the deep color of indigo. I stopped.

What if another year passed before I saw Cole again? What if I never saw him again? He was like a firefly, blinking bright in my life one minute and vanishing the next. I needed him to remember *everything* about me.

I faced him. My breath shortened. He stood by the railing watching me, his hands at his sides. The overhead dock-lamp glowed on his gold-streaked hair and carved his strong features into planes of shadows and light.

A flame lit beneath my heart. I might not have this chance ever again. I ran back to him and threw my arms around his neck. Our gazes crashed, hot and crackling. His eyes widened. I gripped the back of his neck, pulled him down to me, and pressed my lips against his.

Oh my God. Heat soared through me. My pulse raced, excitement ricocheting in my veins like a thousand pinballs, lights flashing, bells and whistles resounding.

Cole stiffened in shock. I drove my hands into his thick hair, deepening the kiss. Then resistance appeared to snap inside him, like a taut wire breaking. He brought his hands up to either side of my head, his grip strong and certain. The pressure of his mouth increased as he not only responded to my kiss, but *took control.*

He urged my lips apart with his, slipped his tongue into my mouth, tightened his hold on me with a sudden desperation that cemented my certainty and trust in him. The combined tastes of cherry and pineapple flooded me. He smelled like salt, the sun, the forest. My breasts crushed against his solid chest. His lower body pressed against mine, a distinct hardness in his jeans throbbing against my belly. Dizziness swept through my head. Oh, he was so warm and strong, his body heat inciting a fire in my blood.

At some purely primal level, I knew this was *it*, that whatever my future held in the way of romantic kisses, I would always compare them to this one.

No. I didn't want to compare any other man's kisses to Cole's. I only wanted *him*.

I broke away, breathless and hot. He released me as if he'd just been burned by a stove. His chest heaved. Lust darkened his eyes. Sparks and electricity charged the air.

"Would you..." I swallowed to ease the dryness in my throat. "Would you like to have coffee sometime?"

A shutter descended over his expression, wiping out the desire. My heart began a slow drop to the pit of my stomach.

"I'm sorry, Josie." He averted his gaze, rubbing the back of his neck. "No."

He turned and strode away, his shoulders stiff. Within seconds, he'd disappeared into the crowd and was gone.

CHAPTER 2

Cole

J osie Mays.

Flopping onto the bed, I closed my eyes and threw an arm over my face as if darkness could block her out.

Hah. She was only more vivid—straight dark hair falling past her shoulders, her goddamned perfect body in a *Save the Bumblebee* T-shirt and denim shorts. She'd always worn clothes that were just a little too big for her, but nothing could hide the tempting curves of her breasts, her round hips and ass, those long legs I'd give anything to open up.

Less than an hour after she'd blindsided me with a kiss that made the earth tilt, I was still hard. I could still feel my dick pushing against Josie's belly while she thrust her tongue into my mouth and gripped my hair. Fucking hell if my world hadn't condensed to *her*—cherries, coconut sunscreen, impossibly soft body that molded against mine as if she'd been made for me.

Of course she had.

No. That thought couldn't see the light of day. I shoved it back down deep. It slithered up again, taunting and cold.

You fucking fool. Josie's had you wrapped around her little finger for over ten years, and now she has you so tangled up you'll never find your way out.

Sweat trickled down my chest. With effort, I suppressed all the fantasies straining to break free. Josie spread naked on my bed, eyes wide and skin flushed pink. Josie on top of me, little gasps coming from her throat, clawing her fingernails into my chest.

Stop.

Dragging in a breath, I swung my legs to the floor. The air was thick, the oscillating fan in the corner not doing much to cool the tiny room I rented above a boathouse. I pushed the single window open farther. Dock lights illuminated the boats clustered at the harbor, and in the distance, the carnival lights spun and twinkled at the pier.

I had to get out of here. Not just this room, but out of Castille altogether. One more year, and I would. Almost a dozen years here was long enough.

I'd been eleven when my asshole father moved his company to Castille. Iron Horse Brewery had been an immediate hit, and my father had become close friends with the mayor, Edward King, as well as the chief of police and lieutenants, the city council members, all of the prominent business owners.

He invited them for poker games, three-martini lunches, golf dates. He donated to their pet causes, sponsored school district fundraisers, supported their initiatives. He was in tight with them, and the town loved him for it.

Just one reason why they'd never investigated him. No one believed Kevin Danforth capable of holding a cigarette lighter close enough to his son's eye to singe his lashes. Or putting a knife to his wife's throat and threatening to kill her. Or locking them both in a closet and announcing he was going to set the house on fire. Or forcing his wife into an institution and driving her to suicide.

In that, he was smart. Often just short of being violent, there was never any physical evidence of abuse, even if anyone had bothered to investigate. No one had. Not a single person of authority—the police, social workers, child protective services—had done a damned thing. They'd refused to reconcile a boy's allegations of an enraged father with the charismatic, successful Kevin Danforth of Iron Horse Brewery.

I'd thought I could get away from him when I turned eighteen. In some ways I had, but I'd been forced to stay in Castille. I'd cut off all contact with my father and stopped working at the brewpub, but I'd had shitty high-school grades and a juvenile delinquency record that a judge—one of my father's poker buddies—had refused to seal when I turned eighteen.

Ford's College had been the only place to offer me conditional admission. If I enrolled in certain courses, maintained a good GPA, and completed work-study programs, they would let me in.

I'd jumped at the chance. Ford's had an exceptional Marine Sciences program, and for the first time in my life, I'd envisioned the possibility of a future studying ocean conservation.

Now I was heading into my fifth year of a full course load and two jobs. One more year of ass-busting work, and I'd graduate. After that, I planned to apply for work at the Marine Science Institute in New York.

Then I'd get out of this godforsaken town for good. Leave Kevin Danforth in the dust where he belonged.

I grabbed a soda from the fridge and headed outside where the air was cooler and smelled like salt. The Castille Harbor stretched out beside a park and playground. Houses clustered the area leading to downtown.

A tree-dotted hill sloped toward the opposite end of the cove, indicating the town's southern boundary. Though teenagers sometimes climbed the hill for clandestine drinking parties, it was deserted aside from a lopsided little cottage that Josie's father had built for her mother to use as an art studio. Sometimes I saw the cottage lights on at night, but usually the hill was dark. I pulled a rusted lawn chair to the dock and sat, opening the cold soda. The night air cooled my heat a little.

Josie Mays. She'd always been the one person who never thought I *was* my shitty reputation. In fact, she'd always seemed to like me. As kids, I'd found her cute but pesky, and in high school she'd stood apart from her giggly friends with a quiet observance that made me think she could see right through me. If I let her.

And now she was a stunning, green-eyed young woman who tasted like cherries and whose curvy body fit so perfectly against mine...

No. I wouldn't let myself think about Josie as she was now, but I'd never forget the first time she rescued me.

CHAPTER 3

Cole

Eleven years ago

"A re you lost?" A girl's voice broke the silence of the woods. I looked up from my crouched position by the tree, slamming the world atlas closed in front of me. A skinny dark-haired girl, maybe seven or eight, in a faded Scooby-Doo T-shirt and worn shorts stood nearby, her fingers hooked in the straps of a red backpack.

I scowled. She blinked.

"You're lost." She gestured to the dense woods around us.

"I'm not lost."

She fisted her hands on her hips. "Then what are you doing here?"

"None of your business." I got to my feet. I was tall for an eleven-year-old, and I stepped toward her to intimidate her with my superior size. "What are *you* doing here?"

"I cut through the woods on my way home from school sometimes. I look for injured squirrels or birds. I take them home and my dad calls the wildlife people so we know what to do. If you want, you can come with me."

"No, thanks."

She regarded me frankly. "Who are you?"

"Cole."

"I'm Josie." She took off her backpack and dropped it to the ground. "Well, Josephine. But only when my mom's mad. Which isn't often. So mostly I'm just Josie."

"Whatever." I sank back down beside the tree trunk.

"You're Cole like the black stuff my dad uses to make burgers?"

"What? No. It's C-o-l-e, not c-o-a-l."

"Oh." She scratched her head. Her ponytail was falling out. "Do you go to Castille Elementary?"

"Yeah." Because of the small class sizes, the elementary and middle schools in this town were combined. Which meant everyone knew everyone else and you couldn't get away from teachers who had you pegged as a bad kid.

"What grade?" She unzipped her backpack. It was bright red with yellow daisies and the name JOSIE printed in blue letters. Really dumb looking.

"Fifth."

"I'm in third." She started taking stuff out of her backpack—a plastic bag of books, a notebook, a worn stuffed rabbit with floppy ears. "My teacher is Miss Henderson. She's nice. We read books about birds sometimes and eat graham crackers."

"Good for you."

"This is Wally." She waved the old rabbit at me. "He goes everywhere with me."

"Whatever."

"What's that?" She indicated the worn atlas.

"A book of maps."

"Cool. I like maps. Italy looks like a boot."

She didn't seem to care that I didn't want to talk to her. She finally pulled a plastic bag of crumbly goldfish crackers out of her backpack and sat cross-legged beside me.

"Want one?" She held the bag out.

Though I was starving—my mother had forgotten to give me lunch money, which happened often—I shook my head.

She ate a cracker. "How come I've never seen you?"

"We moved here a couple weeks ago."

"You mean your family?"

I scowled again. "Yeah. What'd you think I meant?"

She shrugged. "Where do you live?"

"I don't know. A house. I don't know the street."

"I live at 546 Poppy Lane. I have an older sister named Vanessa. My mom is an artist. My dad works at the post office and writes books about history. He's the president of the Castille Historical Society. And sometimes he delivers the mail. Sometimes he just sorts it out. I've gone with him to work a few times. It's fun."

Fun. Envy stabbed me. I'd never had fun with my father. Never would.

I rolled my eyes to show her I didn't care.

"Do you like to fish?" she asked.

"I don't know."

"Swim?"

Swimming was one of the only things I liked. When we first moved to Castille, I'd found an isolated little swimming hole where I could go whenever I wanted. One of the few bearable things about having Kevin Danforth as a father was that he didn't pay attention to where I was—if I wasn't supposed to be at school or the brewery.

"I like to swim," I said.

"We play Kick The Can sometimes on our street. You could come, if you want."

"Never played it."

"I could show you."

"No thanks."

She finally shut up. The only sounds were the birds and Josie crunching goldfish crackers. When she'd finished the bag, she crumpled it up and stuffed it into her pocket.

"So, you want to come with me?" She started putting her crap back into her backpack. "I'm going to look for more animals and then get an ice cream."

"You seem a little young to be running around by yourself."

"I'm not running. I'm walking."

"Whatever."

"Usually Vanessa walks home with me, but she had track after school." She hitched her backpack onto her shoulders. It was too big for her, making her look like a turtle. "Sure you don't want to come with me?"

She was...what? Seven? I couldn't let her wander around the woods all by herself. What if a serial killer was hiding in the bushes?

Slowly I got to my feet again and picked up my backpack. "Well, okay. But only because you could get lost."

"Oh, I never get lost." She lifted her chin. "I come out here all the time with my dad. Camping and hiking and stuff. It's easy once you know the way."

"Whatever."

She started marching off like she actually did know the way. As I started after her, my foot kicked a ratty, polka-dot notebook that she'd taken out of her backpack. The pages were open, fluttering in the slight breeze. I picked it up and glanced over the drawings of animals—foxes, badgers, raccoons, moose, owls. All with little accessories, like hats, canes, and scarves.

I guessed they were okay drawings for a little kid.

"You forgot your book." I glanced in the direction she'd gone, but she was nowhere to be seen.

Unease hit me. Either she really was fast, or she'd gotten abducted.

"Hey!" What was her name again?

Slinging my pack over my shoulder, I hurried after her. I caught a glimpse of her bright red backpack and swinging pony-tail through the trees. I blew out a relieved breath. She was just too small to be out here by herself.

"Hey, you forgot this!" I called.

She stopped and turned, rolling her eyes. "Oh geez. That's my storybook about Mr. Peddler and Ms. Nutbaum. Thanks."

She tucked the notebook into her backpack and started walking again. I followed and let her lead me out of the woods, where I'd definitely been lost.

CHAPTER 4

Josie

"And not only did he walk away after kissing me like he was starving and I was an entire chocolate cake *with frosting...*" I spread my arms out in remembered outrage "...but he rejected my coffee invitation, of all things. *Coffee*, Vanessa. I didn't propose marriage."

"Well." My sister eyed me with speculation as she twisted a lock of thick blonde hair around her forefinger. "I realize dating has never been your thing, but protocol dictates that the coffee date comes *before* the hot kiss."

"I know." I groaned and flopped back on the white sofa in her condo living room. For the past week, I hadn't been able to stop thinking about Cole. "That's the problem. I totally screwed it up and scared him away. If I try and contact him through the student directory, he'll think I'm stalking him."

"Are you sure he doesn't have a girlfriend?"

"No, of course I'm not sure. But as far as I know, he didn't have any girlfriends in high school."

"He's been in college for four years." Vanessa arched a delicately plucked eyebrow. "If he's as hot as you say, then he's definitely had girlfriends."

"God." I put my hands over my face, embarrassment rising to my cheeks. "What was I thinking? He's always seen me as a helpless little squirrel he'd found in the woods. Now that I'm in college, I think I've suddenly transformed into a swan? And that Cole Danforth will get all googly-eyed and tongue-tied at the sight of my beauty? I mean, I was wearing torn jean shorts and my *Save the Bumblebee* T-shirt. I had zero makeup and probably ketchup on my chin."

"Okay, first of all you're not allowed to have a pity party." Vanessa lifted her hands, her expression sympathetic. "And second, Cole was a troubled kid. His mother had serious mental issues, and obviously that affected him. You can't blame his twitchiness on anything *you* did when he's got a whole cart full of baggage. Cut him some slack and try another approach. I would, however, not recommend flinging yourself at him again for an impromptu lip-lock."

"I'm not sorry I did it." I rose onto my elbows to look at her. "It was really hot, and I swear to you he kissed me back. But I realize I freaked him out. So if he won't have a stupid cup of coffee with me, what am I supposed to do?"

"Find a connection, something you remember from when you were kids. Meet him on his own territory so he feels like he's the one in control."

"The first time we met, he was looking at an atlas. He used to love maps." I scrunched my forehead. "Am I supposed to go over to the Marine Sciences building and bring him a map? He'll think I'm such a dork."

"Doesn't he already?" Amusement filled my sister's eyes.

"Thanks, Homecoming Queen."

She laughed and approached me. "Josie, that's probably why he's always kind of looked out for you. Why he likes you. You're this super cute, dorky little artist who always has paint on her clothes. He wants to take care of you."

"Then why did he walk away?"

"Ask him." She squeezed my shoulder in comfort and picked up the empty popcorn bowl I'd left on the table. "You're over-thinking this. You and Cole already know each other, so that's half the battle. Do you know where he hangs out besides school and the pier?"

"He said he swims at some section of Eagle Canyon, but that place is huge. I wouldn't know where to begin looking for him." I bit my lip. "He said it's hard to reach, which is why he goes there."

A thought struck me. "He said it was near some stone ruins. But I don't know of any ruins in Eagle Canyon."

"There used to be an old stone tower off Spiral Pass." Vanessa brought the bowl into the kitchen, calling over her shoulder. "I remember Dad talking about it once when it was on the Historical Society agenda. I guess they took it off the preservation list or whatever because it was falling apart and they didn't have the money to reconstruct it."

"Where is it?" I took out my phone and searched for *Spiral Pass*. "It's not on the map."

"It's just a pile of rubble now." Vanessa returned and held out her hand for my phone. "We stopped there once on the way to the cabin when I was around fourteen. I can't remember any swimming hole, though. Here."

She pointed to a narrow, barely visible road off the winding Spiral Pass.

"Should I just show up?" I asked.

"Why not? He might not even be there." She sat back down at her desk. "Then again, he might. Just don't wander too far by yourself, and be sure you have your phone with you."

"There's no signal that far up Eagle Canyon."

"There's a clear spot where those ruins are," Vanessa said. "Dad called one of the Historical Society people when we stopped there. They had this ridiculously long conversation about erosion and crumbling mortar. I was so bored."

Though my chances of actually finding Cole at the tower ruins were slim, I saw no reason not to give it a shot. Even if I didn't see him, I could spend the weekend at the cabin and do some sketching. I shoved my phone back into my pocket and sat up.

"I have to get to work in half an hour. What else did you want to talk about?"

"Mom and Dad's twenty-fifth anniversary is next June." Vanessa opened her floral planner and studied a page of notes. "They have their trip to Europe planned, but I was thinking we could throw them a surprise party. Like a big, all-out, once-in-a-lifetime bash with everyone we know. We could have a catered dinner, cake, disc jockey, the whole works."

"That's a great idea. Where would we have it?"

"The Seagull Inn has that big room they rent out for private parties. It's available the Saturday night before Mom and Dad leave for Europe, so I went ahead and booked it."

"I can paint signs and get photo posters made." I snapped my fingers. "Oh, one of my fellow students is also a roaming magician. He does parties and stuff all the time. I can ask him to come. And since we'll probably have a lot of families there, we could even do face painting and maybe a balloon artist."

"Awesome." Anticipation lit in her eyes. "Can you look into hiring people for that stuff? I'll start checking out caterers and DJs."

"Sure." I pulled on my beat-up leather boots and stood. "You think we should plan this far in advance? It's a full year."

"I know, but June is prime wedding season, and everyone gets booked up really early. We need to get things scheduled now."

"Okay." I headed to the door. "I'll let you know what I find out."

"Don't forget Mom's art exhibit opening Friday night," Vanessa called after me. "Want me to pick you up?"

"Sure. I'm taking Teddy to see the new *Avengers* movie Friday afternoon, so he'll be with me." Our twelve-year-old brother had yet to outgrow superheroes, much to my delight. "Just text me what time we should be ready."

Vanessa eyed me warily, raking her gaze over my torn jeans and *Free Spirit* T-shirt. "And what do you intend to wear, sister of mine?"

"Uh...something nice?"

Vanessa crossed her arms and gave me her *"how are we sisters?"* look. It was true that we were like salt and pepper—of the same family, but very different.

Aside from our different social statuses, Vanessa paid attention to things like color highlights and manicures. She worked for an interior design firm and lived in a beautiful, shabby chic condo. I wore paint-spattered jeans, chewed my fingernails, and lived in a shoebox apartment crammed with garage-sale furniture and art supplies.

"I'll wear the red jersey dress," I assured my sister.

"Okay. Don't forget lipstick."

I hustled myself out of there before she could remind me about mascara too.

❧

Sucking on a red gummy bear, I drove up the narrow, winding road ascending Eagle Mountain. Trees blanketed either side of the pass, with several precarious ledges jutting over the canyon. Far below, a river flowed through the steep rock formations, creating multiple waterfalls and swimming holes.

Ever since I could remember, our family had spent many

summer weekends at the cabin nestled deep in the mountain. Heavenly Daze, my father had named it. The lack of TV and cell phone signals allowed us to do all the things he loved—hiking, fishing, campfires, board games, reading.

The road Vanessa had told me led to the ruins was almost unnoticeable, a single dirt lane whose entrance was half-covered by brush. I eased my car off Spiral Pass and followed the road. The ruins weren't far from the pass, a pile of huge stones arranged in a semi-circle. Beside them was a beat-up old Ford, which just might...

My insides tightened. It was a hot Saturday afternoon, perfect for swimming, so it was entirely possible the car belonged to someone else. It wasn't as if this were private property.

I parked and grabbed my backpack. The sound of rushing water filtered through the trees. Birds twittered, and squirrels rustled through the undergrowth.

I passed the ruins and headed in the direction of the canyon, pushing aside branches and prickly bushes. My flip-flops slipped on the loose rocks. I reached the tree line and peered toward the canyon. High cliffs extended over the river, the striated rocks tumbling into the water. Waterfalls spilled down the opposite side into a wide pool sparkling with sunlight.

And there...

God in heaven.

Cole was climbing up the embankment to a large, flat boulder jutting at least twenty feet above the water. Wearing only a pair of swimming trunks, he took my breath away—his muscles flexing and straining, his wet hair darkened to copper, his naked, golden-brown tanned skin glistening with water droplets.

I grabbed a nearby tree trunk. My heart hammered. This was a stupid idea. Vanessa knew a hell of a lot more about men than I did, but...really? I was stalking him, invading his privacy.

He looked up, his eyes narrowing on the trees as if he sensed me. Our gazes crashed together like metal striking stone. The air sparked. Tension coiled in my belly.

No chance of hiding now.

I crept out from behind a tree and gave him a tentative wave and a smile, as if I'd just happened upon him while hiking through the forest.

"Hi there," I called.

He grabbed a handhold on a boulder and hauled himself up to the cliff's plateau. The sun beamed down on him like he was the Chosen One, glittering off his bronzed skin and caressing his well-defined muscles.

In all my art history studies, I'd never seen a sculpture that rivaled Cole Danforth's half-naked beauty. Everything inside me responded to him, tightening and pulsing.

Irritation creased his forehead. "What are you doing here?"

"Just passing by," I replied cheerily. "Um, I guess I'll be going now."

"Josie." His voice deepened into a reprimand that sent an unexpected tingle down my spine.

"Okay." With a sigh, I edged my way uneasily down the rocky incline to the boulder. "When you told me about finding a swimming hole near some ruins, I figured out what you meant. My family has a cabin not far from here, so I wanted to see what you were talking about."

He planted his hands on his hips and looked past my shoulder. "Are you alone?"

"Yes."

"You shouldn't be." A frown tugged at his mouth. "It's not safe for you to hike through the canyon alone."

"Well, *you're* here," I pointed out.

His eyes darkened. "That might put you in more danger."

My heart crashed against my ribs. I would have very much liked to be *in danger* with Cole Danforth, though not the kind he was talking about.

"I'm not afraid of you," I said. "I never have been, no matter what people have said about you."

He studied me implacably for a second before turning away. "Go home, Josie."

"This is a really beautiful place." I cast a glance to the cliffs on the opposite side of the canyon, where the rock face was a nearly vertical drop to the river. "How often do you come here?"

"Whenever I can."

"It's not safe for you to be here alone either."

"*Alone* is the only place I've ever been safe."

Startled, I turned to stare at him. Consternation tightened his features. I had the sudden sense that whatever I said next would be a turning point for us—either he would come closer or retreat. Maybe for good this time.

Anxiety lit in my veins.

"In 1596," I said. "Gerardus Mercator invented some sort of mapping technique that greatly improved sea voyage navigation."

Cole blinked.

"And in the 1950s, oceanographer Marie Tharp drew the first detailed map of the North Atlantic Ocean floor," I continued, keeping my gaze nervously on him. "The great white shark has to breathe with some kind of technique that I forgot the name of, but he'll die from lack of oxygen if he stops moving."

Silence. The sun continued to shine on him, drying the last drops of water clinging to his smooth shoulders. In the bright light, his eyes were astonishingly blue, flecked with gold like little flames.

A strange feeling settled in my heart—a kind of growing and shrinking at the same time, like I was blowing up a balloon and had to keep stopping to take a breath.

"Obligate ram ventilation," he said. "I told you that."

I nodded. Whenever we'd crossed paths in the woods as kids, I'd fallen into step beside him as if it were a given that we'd walk to or from school together. We'd never stayed together for long,

usually because he hurried on ahead or diverted toward downtown, but every so often we'd had a conversation long enough for
him to divulge some bit of trivia that my young mind had stored
away like a chipmunk hoarding precious acorns.

"I remembered everything you told me." Deciding it was now
or never, I took my courage in both hands. I hadn't followed him
to the top of a cliff to back off now.

"I always felt a bit different from the other kids," I explained.
"Especially compared to my sister. She was so smart and pretty,
and she had this big circle of friends and admirers...she *fit*, you
know? I was fine with being her weird little sister...I still am...
but I was still often off by myself, drawing or rescuing birds and
squirrels.

"So when I first met you, I was fascinated because you were
also different, but you didn't seem to care. You knew all these
obscure little facts. You didn't mind hanging out with a girl three
years younger. You liked being in the woods as much as I did.
You didn't try and act like someone you weren't, not even with
teachers and other students. You were just...*you*. And I admired
you so much."

He didn't move. Tension laced his shoulders. His blue-sea
eyes didn't leave mine.

I swallowed hard. *Will he come closer or...?*

He took a step toward me. Then a couple more until he was
standing in front of me. My vision filled with the sun-soaked,
bronzed reality of Cole Danforth so close I could see the ring of
indigo surrounding his irises and the pulse beating at the hollow
of his throat.

"When I found this place," he said slowly, "I was running away
from home because my father is a vindictive bastard and a liar."

I'd never heard him mention his father. A strange mixture of
outrage and hope twisted through me.

"Why?" I whispered.

"He was abusive...physically violent and threatening, but even

worse, he was a manipulator. A gaslighter." His tone roughened
with anger. "After twenty years of marriage, he had my mother
convinced she was crazy. She wasn't. But he had her go on
medication and kept fucking with her head enough that she
thought she was. It was the reason she wouldn't leave, not even
when I begged her. She'd tell me my father was a good man, that
he only wanted what was best for us. Sometimes I thought she
actually believed it."

I couldn't speak past the constriction in my throat. I sensed
this unfolding of Cole's secrets would change everything
between us.

"I ran away a few times, but I always went back because I
didn't want to leave her alone with him." Pain darkened his eyes.
"I thought if I was there, I could protect her. Sometimes I did...if
he was hitting me, he wasn't hitting her. When I was a junior in
high school, he blamed her for a failed investment he'd wanted to
open a new brewpub. He accused her of screwing it up, said she
was sleeping with the investor...all this shit that made no sense.
Of course, she denied it, he kept pushing...then finally she
wondered if it *was* her fault. He told her she needed professional
help. She didn't want to go to an institution, so he went to court
and had her committed. She was there for seven months. The
first week she was home, she killed herself."

"Oh, Cole." I pressed my hands to my face. A tangled mess of
anger and sorrow flooded my chest. I recalled hearing that he
had been the one to find his mother's body when he'd gotten
home from school. "I'm so sorry."

"Sometimes I even wished she really was crazy." He stepped
away, flexing his hands. "At least then he couldn't have fucked
with her so much. I might have been able to protect her too."

"It wasn't your fault. You have to know that."

He shrugged, his jaw tightening. "Maybe it was. I should have
done more to alert the authorities about what a fucking asshole
he is."

"Did you try?"

"Yeah. But he has the whole town conned. The district court judge and police chief are two of his closest buddies. He has everyone believing he has a share in a royal Bavarian brewing company dating to the seventeenth century. Hell, every Christmas he still sends the whole police department packages of all his goddamned craft brews. He knows how to work them. So the police, the teachers, whoever...they took his side."

He flexed his hands again. "It's why I've always hated it here. All that bullshit about what a great guy Kevin Danforth is. Poor man, stuck with a crazy wife and a loser kid who did nothing but cause problems for him. When I tried to tell them the truth, they didn't believe me."

"I believe you."

Sudden tension rolled through him. He tracked his gaze over my face, his forehead creased.

"You were..." His throat worked with a swallow. "You were like this little woodland *elf* I saw every now and then. You always seemed happy, you know? With your red backpack and ponytail. I was kind of bummed when I started high school and had to take a different route. I missed running into you."

A bubble lifted beneath my heart, shiny and translucent. "It was the same for me, except you were more like a mysterious enigma than an elf." I frowned slightly. "I'm not sure I love the *elf* comparison anyway, but whatever. I liked seeing you too. And I *really* like seeing you again now."

The cloud dimming his eyes lifted a little. Not entirely, but as if the storm was starting to break.

He moved closer. My breath stuck in the middle of my throat. Despite his dark history, he glittered with light and heat. This beautiful boy with gold-streaked hair and ocean eyes belonged in the woods, the water, anywhere he could drink in the sun-filled air.

He lifted a hand to the side of my face, cupping my cheek like a cradle. My heart grew wings, fluttering with nervous, wild abandon. He tilted my chin up and brought his mouth down on mine.

And, *oh,* if the forest itself didn't dance and whirl around us. His kiss was gentle, almost hesitating, his lips moving with near caution over mine before he brought his hand to the other side of my face.

I parted my lips. Our tongues met with a spark that shot clear down to my toes. The taste of him—fresh water and peppermint —filled my blood with warmth. I eased closer still, nudging my breasts against his chest. Arousal began a low, throbbing pulse in my core.

The waterfalls applauded. The birds chirped their approval. The squirrels frolicked. The wind rustled music through the trees.

If *this* wasn't falling in love, then I never wanted to know what was. Surely nothing in the universe, no matter how rich or complex, could be better than this feeling of pure, total joy and hope.

Cole lifted his head. Tender warmth softened his eyes. The clouds were gone, leaving nothing but bright blue.

"When I was eleven, if you'd told me that years later, I'd be kissing the all-grown-up little girl in the Scooby-Doo T-shirt, I'd have thought you were joking."

"That's why I didn't tell you." I tapped his nose, easing away from him to glance at the canyon. "How long were you planning to stay here?"

"Couple hours. I have to work tonight." He moved to the cliff's edge and peered down at the river. "Do you want to swim?"

"I didn't bring a suit." My stomach tensed. He was less than a foot away from the drop. "Uh, what are you doing?"

"This is a great place to jump."

Oh hell no.

"Are you kidding me right now?" I hurried toward him as far

as I dared, stopping a good ten feet from the cliff's edge. "That is so dangerous."

"I've done it a bunch of times. It's plenty deep, and the ledge is far enough out that the rocks aren't a danger." He turned, his eyes twinkling, and extended his hand. "Come on, Josie. I seem to recall you're pretty impulsive."

I flushed at the reminder of how I'd kissed him. "Not about this. Remember I don't like heights? I can't even go on the Ferris wheel."

"This isn't the Ferris wheel."

"No, it's a twenty-foot drop to certain death."

"It's an exhilarating, twenty-foot leap into a very deep pool of cold, refreshing river water."

I narrowed my eyes. "Well, when you put it that way..."

"If birds are your favorite animal, you should like to fly."

"That's not flying. It's falling."

"If the landing is safe, falling can be fun too."

Like *falling in love.*

What if I landed right in Cole Danforth's arms? His heart?

I took a breath. Time stretched. His big, strong hand was still extended toward me. Now it was my turn to decide whether to move closer or retreat.

Squashing a wave of outright fear, I slipped out of my flip-flops and unbuttoned my jeans shorts. Cole's gaze tracked my movements as I pulled them off and tugged my T-shirt down over my panties.

I took a few steps closer and slipped my hand into his. Thick calluses roughened his palm.

"Don't let go," I said.

"I won't."

I tightened my grip on his hand. My knees shook. A thousand fears raced through my head. *I'd hit a rock, we'd get pulled under, we'd miss the water entirely, we'd get sucked into an underwater cave...*

Or we'd fly.

We inched toward the edge. My heart almost pounded out of my chest. We stopped when our toes poked just over the rocks.

Our eyes met.

"Count of three?" he asked.

I nodded.

"One two...three!"

We leapt off the cliff. For an instant, I was suspended in midair with Cole beside me. A scream lodged in my chest. We fell, tumbling through air, sunshine, mist, until we hit the water in a vortex of icy cold waves.

He didn't let go. Not when we leapt. Not when we fell. Not when the river submerged us, pulling us downward. He tugged my hand and kicked to the surface, a much stronger swimmer than I was. We broke through with exhilarated gasps and laughter, water pearling on our skin.

"Good job, Josie Bird."

He grinned, quick as a flash. My breath caught. I'd rarely seen him smile, much less display a wide, striking grin that creased his eyes at the corners and made a dimple pop into his left cheek.

In that instant, my heart knew the truth. If Cole Danforth would rescue me from mean boys, tell me his secrets, and hold my hand through a jump from a twenty-foot cliff, then nothing could ever force him to let go.

Nothing.

CHAPTER 5

Josie

An hour later, Cole and I stretched out on the rocks, toasting in the sun. A warm, languid sensation spread through my veins. The heat had dried my T-shirt and underwear within a few minutes. I turned to face him, tucking my hands under my head.

"Why Marine Sciences?" I asked.

"My grandfather was a marine biologist." He rose to a sitting position and reached for his backpack. "My mother's father. He was a professor at Columbia. Did a lot of work on the physics and biology of oceans. He gave me my first books about marine life. He died when I was seven, but I was fascinated by his stories and knowledge. Guess it stayed with me."

"Do you have any other relatives?"

"My mother's brother lives down in New York. He's a good guy." A shadow crossed his face. "Never saw much of him, though. My mother didn't want to. I think she was scared he might find out about my father."

He shook his head, as if to dislodge old memories. Not wanting him to go back into the darkness, I pointed to a little gray-and-brown bird hopping nearby.

"That's a boreal chickadee. They eat and store spruce seeds."

"The black-capped chickadee is the Maine state bird." He lifted his eyebrows at my surprised glance. "I know a thing or two."

"That's why I like you."

His mouth curved into a smile. A warm current passed between us, settling in my lower body. Not even the cold river water had mitigated the heat simmering inside me, a direct result of everything about this moment. Cole's muscular, tanned body so close to mine, the sun on my bare skin, the rub of my tight nipples against my bra and T-shirt...which I'd caught Cole glancing at more than once.

I let out my breath slowly. I'd fooled around with a few boys in the past, but I was still a virgin, a fact I was neither embarrassed about nor proud of. My mother had never put much importance on "virginity," believing it contributed to social biases about female purity and commodification of women.

While I could appreciate her intellectual sentiments, my personal reason for still being a virgin was the simple fact that I'd never been so attracted to a boy that I wanted to have sex with him.

Until now.

Surreptitiously, I eyed the length of Cole's strong legs, his hair-roughened thighs corded with muscle. He rested his hand on the rock beside him. What would his callused palm feel like sliding over my breasts, my nipples, my belly? What if he slipped his hand between my thighs, opening them up so he could delve his long fingers right into my—

A breeze tickled my nose. I sneezed. My little fantasy broke apart. Cole rummaged through his backpack and produced a thick, soft tissue that felt like velvet.

I wiped my nose, rubbing the tissue between my fingers. "What is this luxurious product?"

"No idea. I grabbed some tissues from a box at the boathouse."

"It must have lotion. I never buy tissues with lotion, but I love them. They even have some with aloe and vitamin E. I bet this is one of those."

He held out a wad of tissues. "You want the rest of them?"

"How sweet. Your first gift to me."

"Ah, you forgot about the perfect pinecone."

Puzzled, I tried to think. "What pinecone?"

"Once you were in the woods looking for pinecones to make bird feeders. You were about ten years old, and you were upset because you said they were all either smashed or shaped wrong. You wanted to find the perfect pinecone, symmetrical and with wide scales so you could put peanut butter and birdseed between them. And I found you the perfect pinecone."

"*Oh.*" My eyes widened. "Of course. Cole Danforth, I swear you had a crush on me like I had one on you. Thirteen-year-old boys don't give perfect pinecones to girls they don't *like.*"

He scowled, a slight flush cresting his cheekbones. "You were *ten.*"

"But I was an adorable woodland elf, remember?" I held up my hands in a promise not to push the issue, even though I couldn't stop smiling.

Cole's scowl eased as he rummaged through his backpack. He pulled out an orange and dug his thumbnail into the skin. The sweet citrus smell filled the air. With methodical grace, he peeled off the rind, exposing the ripe juicy flesh.

Just watching the movement of his long fingers caused my pulse to increase. *Oh, he could fondle and touch me with such delicious expertise...*

He dropped the peel into a bag in his backpack, broke the

orange into sections, and handed me half. I scooted his towel,
which he'd told me to use since I hadn't brought one, back into
the shade of an overhanging rock.

"I don't tan like you." I slipped a wedge of orange into my
mouth. "My mom's the same way. We both have really pale skin
and burn in the sun."

"I saw your mom's exhibit at the museum." Cole moved back
to join me in the shade. "I don't know much about art, but her
paintings were incredible."

I smiled. "She creates works about female empowerment,
mysticism, and spirituality. She's very *centered*, into meditation
and yoga. Which makes it especially interesting that she married
my dad, who works at the post office, writes books about the
seventeenth-century colonization of Castille, and doesn't know
Zen from transcendental."

"I remember your dad once came to my history class in high
school to teach a unit about the history of Maine. He was a great
teacher. It was probably the one time I was actually interested
and did the work."

He bit into an orange slice. A drop of juice trickled down his
chin. I wanted to lick it away. He drew his hand over his mouth
and glanced at me, wariness clouding his expression.

"I've mostly outgrown my teenaged reputation," he said. "But I
still get shit sometimes, especially because my father has made it
known that I've cut him off. Now everyone feels sorry for him
because his horrible, ungrateful son wants nothing to do with
him. I don't care anymore, but I don't want you to get caught in
the middle of any crap."

"I won't." I ate the last section of orange and wiped my fingers
on my bare thigh. "But even if I did, I wouldn't care."

"I would."

My heart softened and tightened at the same time. "You don't
have to worry about protecting me, Cole. Especially from you."

The troubled look in his eyes didn't dissipate. I scooted closer and rested my palm on his shoulder, loving the sensation of his smooth, taut skin. I wanted to explore every inch of him, to run my fingers over his muscular chest, find all the slopes and planes of his body, reach down into his swimming trunks and—

A shiver raced over my skin.

"Listen." I slid my hand down to his chest. "You might be overthinking this. It's okay if we *like* each other and want to have fun together. We can have a summer fling."

He frowned. "I'd never think of you as a *fling*."

"Then how about a *leap?*"

Cole shook his head and laughed. "Oh, you're a leap all right, Josie Mays. For me, a quantum leap forward."

And for me, Cole Danforth was a leap of faith. I didn't know if he'd ever have the same intensity of feelings for me that I did for him, or if anything would come of our future, but I believed in him hard enough to take the chance.

I leaned forward and pressed my lips to his, sticky and sweet from the orange. My blood heated. Restraint wound through him for an instant before he brought his hand to the back of my neck. He eased my mouth open with his. It was a kiss of citrus, sunshine, river water.

I trailed my fingers over his chest, traced the ridges of his abdomen. He slid his hand up my bare thigh and beneath the hem of my T-shirt. Pulse racing, I tugged my shirt up farther to give him easier access. He cupped my breast, rubbing my stiff nipple through my bra, his breath hot and fast against my lips.

"*Maybe* I had a crush on you when I was thirteen," he murmured. "But I definitely have one on you now."

White-capped waves lifted my heart. I arched into his touch, a silent plea. I didn't want this to end, didn't want *us* to stop. A shudder coursed through him. Our kiss deepened in intensity, tongues seeking, lips caressing. He lowered me onto the towel and moved his mouth to my neck, licking the hot hollow of my throat. I closed my eyes, letting myself slip into our growing passion. So easy, this kind of falling.

Warm both inside and out, I drove my hand into his hair and pulled him closer. Our lips clung, retreated, and met again endlessly. I couldn't get enough of touching his sun-drenched skin, the hard ridges of his abdomen, the tempting trail of hair leading down into his swimming trunks.

We pressed our bodies together, his leg settling heavily over mine. Pleasure coiled through me, an infinite spiral. He moved his hand lower, his fingers finding the edge of my panties and slipping beneath the thin material. The instant his forefinger brushed against my folds, I almost bolted upright.

A guttural noise rasped from his throat. He nudged his hips against my thigh, and the hard pressure of his erection sent both my shock and arousal skyrocketing. He settled his mouth over mine again, working his finger gently against me. Every nerve in my body tensed with sweet, aching need.

"God, Cole." I broke my lips from his to pull in a breath. "That feels so good."

I'd touched myself countless times before, but *this* was a thousand sensations spinning me into a whirlwind. The caress of his lips, the weight of his powerful body, the scent of him...I lost myself in the dizzying vortex and never wanted to be found again.

He pressed his lips to my shoulder, biting down on my collarbone. Tension spiraled in my core and tightened, building toward an intense bliss I knew instinctively would be like nothing I'd ever experienced before.

Cole glided his hand down farther, easing one finger, then another, slowly inside me. I shivered. Sudden unease clouded my arousal. I wanted him so badly, and with so much of myself—my heart, my mind, my body. So why was I locking up at the simple penetration of his fingers?

As if sensing my withdrawal, he stopped and pulled his hand away from me. "Christ, Josie, I'm sorry."

"No, it's not you." A hot flush of embarrassment rose to my cheeks.

"I went too fast." Self-disgust darkened his eyes. He moved away from me, tugging my T-shirt back down over my hips, his jaw clenching. "I didn't mean to…you're just so perfect, and touching you is like…what the hell is that movie about the chocolate factory?"

"Willy Wonka?" I didn't know whether to laugh or cry. "Touching me is like being in Willy Wonka's chocolate factory?"

"Yes. I mean, no…goddammit." He shoved a frustrated hand through his hair and expelled a heavy breath. "I mean, it's like being in a place where everything is so sweet and amazing that I never want to leave. A place where dreams come true. You taste so damned good and you feel so incredible that I want to…to dive right into you and stay there forever. I'm so fucking *greedy* for you that it's like—"

"I'm a virgin." The confession popped out. My heart jammed into my throat.

Cole jerked his head around to stare at me. "A virgin."

"That's why I freaked out a little. It had nothing to do with you, I promise." I gathered my courage and rested my hand on his thigh. "Not only do I have a major crush on you, I really *want* you. And even though virginity is a social construct contributing to control of women and—"

"Uh, what?"

"Never mind." I waved a dismissive hand. "My point is that I really want to have sex with you and I just got a little nervous because…well, you're Cole Danforth. I've had a crush on you for a long time. And honestly, the reality of you, of my wish coming true, is a little overwhelming."

A muscle ticked in his jaw. He shook his head, his shoulders tensing. "What if I'm like my father?"

Startled, I drew back. "What are you talking about?"

"He always gave me shit about having inherited my mother's so-called illness." He dragged a hand down his face. "But what if it's the other way around? What if, deep inside, I'm like him?"

"You listen to me." I grabbed his arm, forcing him to look at me. "You are nothing like your father. You never will be. I've known you since we were kids, and I've only ever had the best feelings for you. So don't you dare insult either me or yourself by thinking for one second that your father has any influence on you whatsoever. You got away from him. You're incredibly strong, brave, and resourceful, and if you have one fault it's that you don't believe you're worthy of good things. That you *deserve* them."

He opened his mouth. To prevent him from arguing, I leaned forward to kiss him. Our lips clung for less than a minute before he pulled away, his breathing rapid.

"I'm doing a lousy job of resisting you," he muttered.

"Then stop trying."

He ran his hand over my hair. A shield descended over his features again, like he was closing himself off.

"I'll walk you back to your car." He pushed to his feet and reached for his backpack. "I need to get to work soon."

My throat tightened. I turned to fold the towel. When I glanced up, I caught him staring at me. For an instant, less than a blink, his shield was gone. In its place was an expression of such intense longing and *need* that my heart skipped a thousand beats.

He averted his gaze, a dull flush rising to his cheeks. Hitching his backpack over his shoulder, he started toward the cliff. I followed. A tiny hope nudged through my dismay.

What if I could show him how much he deserved to be loved?

CHAPTER 6

Cole

The sun burned a hole in the sky, radiating off the water. Ten hours at sea, and not for an instant had Josie left my thoughts as I prepped bait, hauled up lobster traps, and sifted through the day's catch. Hard as I found it to believe that she'd be okay with a summer *fling*—and as much as I could never think of her as one—I latched on to the idea like a barnacle.

Because if I lied to myself and got together with her for a *fling*, then I could indulge in her for the next month. And indulge I would, like diving headfirst into a pile of sugary whipped cream or a chocolate river.

Then what happens? You make a mess and don't clean it up. And what if you can't walk away from her at the end of this so-called fling?

I had no idea. That girl was my every weakness. My Achilles' heel, the chink in my armor, my kryptonite. I'd trailed after her when I was eleven. Now I was ready to fall to my knees and *grovel* after her. No matter how many times I told myself to stay away.

It was like I was parched with thirst, dripping with sweat, burned by the sun. Standing at the edge of a cliff, staring down into a pool of cool, fresh water.

How could I resist taking the leap?

Ignoring my apprehension, I finished hosing down the deck just as the boat approached the harbor. After we were moored, I climbed onto the dock and got ready to offload the four hundred pounds of lobster we'd hauled up from the traps.

One by one, we transferred the lobster from the live-tank to a tote, where they were weighed and calculated. I collected my pay —a shitty amount for a full day's work since the price of lobster had decreased. I headed back home to shower and change for a night operating carnival games.

I'd need a third job this year. The Marine Sciences TA and research positions were all given to grad students, but I might be able to find work in the department. Despite my two jobs, I was in significant debt from student loans. Interning at the Marine Institute after graduation wouldn't help relieve my finances. I'd have to reduce my debt before I could even consider applying to grad schools.

As I approached the boathouse, my spine tensed. A tall, bulky man stood at the end of the dock, partly shaded by the harbor sign. Every muscle in my body locked into place. I hadn't seen my father for months.

I stopped, eyeing his craggy features and thinning hair with a hatred I no longer wanted to hide. "What do you want?"

"Hello to you, too."

Fuck you.

I flexed my hands. "I've got stuff to do."

"I just need a minute." He raked his gaze over my dirty jeans and torn T-shirt. "Your twenty-third birthday is coming up."

"And?"

"I expected you to come talk to me about your trust fund."

Right. I'd haul lobster traps until my hands bled before I'd go to my father for my trust fund, a percentage of which was to be doled out to me when I turned twenty-three. The fund had been set up by my paternal grandfather, and my father was the designated trustee. That meant he was the one who ensured the allocation of the money.

Nothing would make me give him that kind of power.

"I don't want my trust fund."

"No?" He lifted his eyebrows. "You're crazier than your mother if you turn down this kind of financial security."

Anger clawed up my chest. I struggled to push it back down, not wanting to give him the satisfaction of knowing he could still get to me.

"Guess I'm a mama's boy, then," I remarked coldly.

He laughed, humorless and rough. "No kidding. I always worried you'd inherited her mental instability."

I wanted to stalk past him, but he was blocking the path to the boathouse. If I got near him, I'd take him down. Much as I wanted to feel his bones cracking under my fists, he'd have me arrested for assault and battery. Knowing his influence with the police and court system...I'd stand no chance. And I sure as hell wouldn't ruin my future for him.

"Look." He held up his hands, as if he was trying to placate me. "I know you're struggling. And this trust fund isn't a couple thousand dollars. It's a significant fortune, funded by shareholder investments your grandfather made. As long as you don't squander it, you'll be set for a very long time, if not life. You can do whatever the hell you want."

Whatever I want. Much as I tried to block it, that phrase slithered past my defenses.

"You can donate it to charity," I said. "Keep it. I don't give a shit."

"What about your girl?"

My blood iced. "What?"

"My lead brewer saw you kissing some little hottie at the pier. Figured she was your new girlfriend. Is it serious?"

Disgust choked my throat. "None of your fucking business."

"Okay. I'm just saying, you could treat her well with this money." He took a folded paper out from beneath his arm and extended it to me.

Hating myself for taking the bait, I grabbed it and opened it. The legal letter outlined the terms of the trust and the allocation of the full amount.

I froze. *Significant fortune.* Three million dollars. The trust was set up to deliver the full amount to me by the time I turned twenty-five.

I crumpled the letter in my fist. I'd had to contend with a shitty, abusive father my whole life. No amount of money could make up for that.

So why don't you throw this fucking letter back at him?

"Take some time and read through the details." My father flicked a hand toward the paper. "Talk to the lawyer. Think about it."

I almost told him to go fuck himself. But the insult stuck in my chest.

He smirked, as if he knew I was waging a sudden internal war. As if he sensed it.

"Stop by my office on your birthday. We'll talk." He strolled away, hands in his pockets. "I look forward to our chat."

Anger burned my veins. I stalked back to the boathouse, the letter clutched in my sweaty fist.

&.

"Jolly Rancher?" Josie's voice, sweet and silky, rubbed right up against my skin.

I turned. The bright, multicolored carnival lights and bustling crowd faded into nothing. All I saw was her—full mouth curved into a tentative smile, leaf-green eyes warmly fixed on me.

"What are you doing here?" I tried to put some force into my voice and failed.

"Waiting for your shift to end." She extended the open bag of Jolly Ranchers. "This is a new bag, so there's plenty of cherry."

I picked out a green apple-flavored candy and unwrapped it.

"You don't like the cherry ones?" Josie asked.

"The only time I want to taste cherry is when I kiss you."

Nice. Flirting is a great way to stay away from her.

My regret vanished when an appealing flush colored her cheeks, and her eyes lit with pleasure. She was so damned cute. And she was good. Sweet and pure. I'd never forget the way she looked at me after I stepped in to get her Halloween candy back. In the ten years since that day, no one else had ever looked at me like that.

"Can we try this again?" She leaned closer and lowered her voice. "I would hate to think I scared you away because of my...cherry."

I couldn't help laughing. "Actually what scares me is how much I like you."

She smiled. "I'm a very safe bet, Cole Danforth. When does your shift end?"

"Another hour. I'll text you when I'm done."

My heart constricted as I watched her walk away. In a pair of blue shorts, her perfect dumpling ass swayed back and forth, and her hair bounced against her shoulders.

"Can I get two games?" a customer asked.

Reluctantly, I turned my attention to him. The minutes couldn't tick by fast enough. By the time my shift ended, I was impatient as all hell.

I'd never felt like this for another woman. I'd only had a few girlfriends, whom I'd probably gone overboard trying to treat well. I hadn't realized until Josie how scared I was that I'd end up like my father. Despite what she'd said to me, what if his evil *was* in my DNA?

Smothering a fresh wave of fear, I texted Josie that I'd meet her at the Ocean Carousel and hurried across the pier. The ride featured over fifty sea creatures—exotic fish, walruses, octopi, sharks, otters, and lobster.

Josie stood at the entrance. When her gaze landed on me, the smile that bloomed over her face hit me right in the heart.

"Hey, you." She pointed her thumb toward the carousel. "Want to take a ride?"

"Only if we ride the whale."

"I was thinking the same thing."

After I stopped at the ticket booth, we climbed onto the carousel. The massive humpbacked whale, sporting a goofy grin, red lipstick, and long eyelashes, was the only creature made for two riders. I helped Josie into the front saddle and got on behind her, closing my thighs around her hips. I nuzzled my nose into her hair that smelled like lemongrass.

The tinny, upbeat calliope music started. But again, the lights and music faded. There was only the softness of Josie's body, her back against my chest, her scent enveloping me. When the ride came to a slow halt and she started to climb off, I wrapped an arm around her waist.

"The ride's done," she said, though she made no move to leave.

"I paid for five." I tightened my arm around her and brushed my lips against her cheek. "But that was a mistake."

"Why?"

"I should have paid for ten."

Ah, that warm, admiring look from her again, like I was someone special.

My chest tightened. Even if I did let myself think of this as more than a fling, I couldn't give her much. The only way I'd have money was if I caved and took the deal for my trust fund. Otherwise I had nothing. I'd make a pittance with only a BA in Marine

Sciences. If I applied to grad school, I'd face another five or six years of student loans and mounting debt.

With any other girl, I wouldn't have even considered the future. But Josie and I had a history. For the first time in my life, a *future* with her seemed possible. Maybe inevitable.

Unless something happened to fuck it up.

The carousel started again, music jingling and lights flashing.

And something always happened to fuck it up.

CHAPTER 7

Cole

Josie's birthday was on July twelfth. I could hardly remember my own birthday—probably because my parents either forgot it or ignored it most of the time—but Josie's had been embedded in my memory for the past ten years.

There wasn't much I could do for her birthday, but I needed to prove I cared about her, even if I was still fooling myself about a stupid fling. If a *fling* meant I wanted to spend every minute with her, couldn't wait to see her again when we were apart, and felt like I was flying ten feet off the ground every time she smiled at me...then, yeah, sure. We were having a *fling*.

I didn't have the money for a fancy restaurant or expensive gift, so I baked her a lemon cake and sang "Happy Birthday." When she blew out the single candle, I made a silent wish alongside hers.

I wish I could have you forever.

❦

Ten Years Ago

"Cole!"

I walked faster. My blisters were rubbed raw and hurt like hell. I needed new sneakers.

"Cole. *Cole!*"

With a sigh, I stopped and turned. Josie chugged toward me, her backpack bouncing and her ponytail flying. She was small, even for a nine-year-old, which was why it made me even madder that those dickwads had been bullying her last Halloween. Like it was cool to pick on a little girl.

Except part of me wished I hadn't rushed in to help her. She'd been bugging me all winter, asking me to come over and build a snow fort (*"super big, like Fort Sumter!"*), have dinner (*"Mom's making some kind of noodle dish that you're supposed to have after skiing but I can't remember what it's called"*), play games (*"We got this super cool game called Mousetrap but we have to play it on the table because Teddy still eats stuff from the floor."*)

I'd turned down every invitation. That hadn't stopped her. She was incredibly annoying.

But I waited for her to catch up to me.

"Come on." Breathless, she stopped and pushed her hair away from her eyes. "I want to show you something."

She ran ahead into the woods. Dropping her backpack to the ground, she grabbed a heavy knotted rope hanging from a tree branch. "My dad and I came out here last weekend and made this. We saw a scarlet tanager. It was really pretty, red and black."

She shimmied up the rope faster than a boy. A platform had been nailed to a few branches, like a little treehouse. Josie tossed the rope down to me. "Come on up."

"We need to get to school."

"It's super solid." She jumped up and down like she was

testing the boards. "We're going to put up a tarp and stuff for a roof next weekend. You can use it whenever you want."

"Come on, Josie." I pointed to my ratty old watch. "We'll be late."

She peered down at me. "What if there were no watches or clocks?"

"We'd tell time by the sun."

"What if it was cloudy?"

"Then we'd always be late. Like we will be unless you get down right now."

She grabbed the rope and slid down, hitting the ground with a thud. "Cool, right?"

"Yeah."

"Race you!" She took off on the path toward downtown, her short little legs taking her out of sight in seconds.

Such a pain.

I picked up her backpack, the bright-red one with huge yellow daisies and the name JOSIE printed in blue letters. When she was wearing it, you could see her from a mile ahead. It was like a neon sign screaming, *"I'm Josie Mays!"*

I trudged the rest of the way to school. Kids filed toward the open doors, talking and laughing in groups. I caught a few glances. Nothing new. Four anonymous complaints had been filed against me already this year, all from people who said I was "threatening." Probably Richard Peterson and his crew.

Looping Josie's backpack over my arm, I stopped at my locker and twisted the combination.

"Mr. Danforth." The vice-principal Mr. Reynolds, a tall skinny man with a graying mustache, paused beside me.

I opened my locker and stepped back to let him search it. This happened at least once a month.

Reynolds pursed his lips and eyed Josie's backpack. "Is there a reason you are in possession of that?"

"Yeah. She left it in the woods, and I—"

"Excuse me?" A suspicious glint appeared in his eyes. "You were in the woods with Josephine Mays?"

"No...I mean, yeah, but..."

He snapped his fingers and extended his hand. I gave him the backpack and turned to my locker.

"Come with me, Mr. Danforth."

Irritation gripped my neck. "What for?"

He leaned closer, his eyes narrowing behind his glasses. "Come. With. Me."

I slammed my locker shut and followed him to the office. He pointed to the front counter in a silent order for me to stand there. He went into his office and picked up his phone.

The two secretaries and admin gave me pointed looks, their mouths set. They didn't even know why I was fucking there.

"Mr. Danforth." Reynolds came out of his office, still holding Josie's backpack. "Are you aware that Miss Mays didn't report to class?"

Alarm flickered in my gut. Much as I hated to admit it, I didn't like the fact that Josie spent so much time alone in the woods. She was always by herself, and she was way too little to be there without someone older to keep an eye on her.

At the same time, the girl knew her way around the forest. She'd been the one to show me the way out.

"I didn't know that," I told Reynolds.

He stared at me. "Can you please explain what you were doing in the woods with Miss Mays?"

My alarm turned into anger. *Can you please explain what the fuck you're implying?*

The secretaries stopped to listen.

"We were walking to school." I curled my hands into fists. "We took a shortcut. She forgot her backpack. I brought it to school."

"Why didn't you give it back to her immediately?"

"She ran ahead of me."

"She ran away from you?"

"She ran *ahead* of me." Tension locked my shoulders. Maybe I should have dropped my gaze, looked deferential, but I couldn't fucking stand the way he was needling me. I stared back at him, my chin up and every muscle ready to fight.

"Oh, there you are." Josie's relieved voice came from the hallway.

Reynolds and I both turned. Josie hurried into the office, her face flushed with exertion.

"I went to your homeroom, but you weren't there yet, then I tried your locker, but you weren't there either, so I came here and...surprise!"

She waved her hands around like she was showing off a new car.

"Josie, where were you?" Reynolds turned to her, his expression shifting from threatening to gentle. "Mrs. Fillmore said you didn't come to class."

"I was looking for Cole." She patted my arm like I was a pet dog. "I knew he had my backpack."

Reynolds slanted his gaze from Josie to me and back again. "And why did you think that?"

"Because we were walking to school and took a shortcut, and I forgot my backpack. I was pretty sure he'd bring it to school. He's very responsible."

She pointed to the sign above the desk, which was one of three printed with the school "positive behavior" words: *Be Responsible. Be Respectful. Be Safe.*

Reynolds narrowed his eyes, but handed her the backpack.

"Mrs. Walker, can you please give Josie a late pass to class?" He put his hand on Josie's shoulder. "Josie, I recommend you walk to school with your sister or other friends and avoid any shortcuts." He pointed to the *Be Safe* sign. "We want to ensure all students are safe."

"Okay." Josie shrugged into her backpack and continued to stand there.

"You may go back to class." Reynolds gave her the late pass.

"What about Cole?"

"I'm dealing with him." He made a shooing motion toward the door. "Hurry, or you'll miss the morning announcements."

Josie eyed him a bit warily and glanced at me. I gave her a short nod. She hesitated, then turned and left the office, looking at me over her shoulder again.

"Listen, Mr. Danforth." Reynolds stepped closer, like he was trying to intimidate me with his size. Hah. He was half the size of my asshole father. "Stay away from that girl. Your father is an upstanding, respected member of this community. I would hate to have to call him with concerns about your behavior. I'm sure you don't want to cause him any trouble either."

No, I didn't want trouble. I just wanted to get my mother and myself out of his fucking house. And that alone was trouble.

"Can I go now?" I finally said.

Reynolds glared at me. "Go. You'll have to take a tardy."

I forced myself to saunter out of the office, even though everything in me wanted to run and run and keep running until I'd left this godforsaken town forever.

I turned down the corridor and started toward my locker again.

"Cole!"

Shit.

"Josie, go away." I spun the combination lock and pulled open the locker door.

"But what happened?" She hurried up beside me, her thumbs hooked into the straps of her backpack. "Why was Mr. Reynolds looking so mad at you?"

"Never mind."

"It wasn't because of me, was it?" Mild horror rose to her eyes over the idea that she'd been the cause of any problems.

I sighed. Part of me kind of appreciated her concern. Not many people were all that concerned about me.

"No," I assured her. "It was just a misunderstanding. Now go back to class."

"Okay." She eyed my locker—books on a wooden shelf I'd built, notebooks in a stack, a plastic pouch filled with extra pens. "Wow. You're like a New Caledonian crow. They make tools out of sticks and stuff, then store them away all neat and tidy for later use."

A laugh rose to my throat. She was as weird as I was, just in a different way.

"See you later." She started to walk away, then turned back. "Hey, I'm having my tenth birthday party this summer at Eagle Canyon. I want to invite you, so can I have your address?"

"I can't go."

Her brow wrinkled. "You don't even know the date."

"Yeah, well, I'm busy." I took a few books from my backpack. "Sorry."

Her hurt silence roared in my ears. When I glanced over my shoulder, she was gone.

The next day, I found a birthday party invitation—red with big yellow daisies—stuffed into my locker. I threw it in the trash.

I started walking to class. Turned back. Before I could think, before anyone could see me, I grabbed the crumpled card from the garbage can and shoved it in my pocket.

I never responded.

CHAPTER 8

Josie

July was hot and busy. Tourists and locals crowded the Water's Edge Pier and the downtown cafés of Lantern Square. Between my summer school session, Cole's two jobs, and his search for a third, we didn't see a lot of each other. But even a few minutes in passing was enough to lighten my heart for the rest of the day.

We texted and talked frequently, though every now and then he still put up a wall—okay, maybe it was more of a *screen*—as if he were trying to convince both of us that this was still temporary.

After a week-long battle of pleading and cajoling, I managed to convince him to join my family for one of our dinner-and-board-game Sunday evenings.

"Answer this riddle," my father said the first time Cole came to our old Colonial house on Poppy Lane. "'*Voiceless it cries, Wingless flutters, Toothless bites, Mouthless mutters.*'"

"The wind," Cole said. "That's from *The Hobbit*."

My father lifted his eyebrows, clearly impressed. "Not bad."

"He used to ask all of Vanessa's boyfriends that riddle." Teddy dug his fork into a plate of spaghetti. "None of them ever got it right. Hey, I have a better one. What do you call a person who never farts in public?"

"A private tutor."

They exchanged grins that cemented a mutual admiration.

Later as my mother and I were cleaning the kitchen, she nudged me in the side and whispered, "You should paint him."

I glanced through to the living room, where my father, Teddy, and Cole were playing a game of cards.

"He's a work of art just as he is."

"But he'd be an incredible model." My mother followed my line of sight. "Do you think he'd model for our figure drawing classes?"

"Mom!" I pinched her arm. "*I* don't want him getting naked in front of an entire classroom."

"Well, aren't you a lobster?" She pushed her glasses back up the bridge of her nose with a slight huff.

"What are you talking about?"

"You're a bit shellfish about your man."

I laughed. *With good reason, thank you.*

I'd waited a long time for Cole Danforth, hardly daring to believe that my longtime crush on him would flourish and grow into...*this*. Bluebells, cotton candy, silver dollars, hummingbirds. The ripe, rich delight of knowing I was wanted.

After one of his Friday night shifts at the carnival, we returned to his room above the boathouse. It was a typical college boy's single with a bed, kitchenette, and a table for both dining and doing homework. It was also surprisingly neat, with his books arranged on a narrow shelf and the bed made. Several boxes of sugary breakfast cereal—one of his weaknesses—sat lined up on the counter.

I kicked off my flip-flops and curled up in a chair while he showered. I gazed at the large world map on the wall, dotted with multicolored pins—all the countries and cities Cole hoped to visit one day. Maybe I could go with him.

"You want to go out?" He emerged from the shower, scrubbing a towel over his wet hair. His worn jeans, slung low on his hips, emphasized his burnished chest, the pectoral muscles sloping down to his tight abdomen whose ridges I wanted to trace with my tongue.

A low pulsing started in my belly. "I want to stay here."

He stilled, his eyes darkening. Slowly he lowered his hands from his hair. "You sure?"

"Oh, I'm sure."

He tossed the towel onto the bed and crossed the room, taking my hands and pulling me right up against him. Our bodies connected. The sensation of his warm, damp skin burned right through my T-shirt and bra, increasing the tension coiling through me.

Cole put his hand against the side of my face, studying me with those sea-blue eyes and that faint expression of disbelief that always made me feel somehow magical.

"Kiss me," I whispered.

He stepped closer, backing me up against the wall. He skimmed his gaze across my lips. My pulse went into overdrive. Butterflies danced inside me the instant before he lowered his mouth to mine. Trapped between the wall and his solid frame, I lost myself in what we'd been and everything we still would be.

He kissed me long and deep, knowing exactly what I liked and how I liked it. He stroked his tongue over mine, nibbled my bottom lip, kissed the corners of my mouth. Tingles of excitement rained through me.

Urgency wrapped around us both. He cupped my breast, twisting my nipple through my thin cotton T-shirt. Beneath his taut skin, his muscles tensed with the onset of lust. He was hard already, the front of his jeans heavy with an unmistakable bulge. Before I could reach for his fly, he pulled the hem of my shirt up.

I lifted my arms and let him strip me—shirt, bra, shorts—until I was only wearing my cotton bikini panties with *Monday* printed in bubble letters across the front. A wave of self-consciousness hit me, but he radiated such *want* that my apprehension quickly eased. He raked his hot gaze appreciatively over my small breasts, the curves of my hips, my bare legs.

"It's Friday." He traced the letters on my panties with the tip of his finger.

"It's…" I twitched at his touch. "It's Monday somewhere. I think."

"It's Monday nowhere." He edged his finger underneath the elastic and between my legs.

A breath caught in my throat. "What about Australia?"

"No."

"Mars?"

He chuckled. "Maybe Venus."

"Oh." I gasped as his finger eased into me. "Do you really care what day of the week it is?"

"Not at all. But for the first time ever, I want to kiss a Monday." A wicked gleam flashed in his eyes, and he went down on his knees in front of me.

My heartbeat accelerated. I braced my hand on his shoulder and let him spread my legs apart. He pressed his lips against the *M* on my panties, the heat of his breath burning through the thin cotton.

He stroked his tongue over the O and the N while easing another finger beneath my panties. I shivered, a flame rising in my blood as my body responded to questing penetration of his touch. He had such a heady effect on me, firing me up from zero to sixty with one kiss or touch.

I tightened my grip on his shoulder and pushed my other hand into his gold-streaked hair. He pulled back to look at me, his eyes hot, his cheekbones cresting with a flush. He stroked me harder, urging my arousal higher and higher. I bucked involuntarily toward him, panting, increasingly desperate.

"Cole, I need you."

"I know you do." He pressed his mouth against my belly button, dipping his tongue into the little indentation.

I fisted his hair, aching to have him inside me. Any previous uncertainty I'd had was gone, conquered by both my intensifying love for him and the explosive heat we generated. He kissed a trail down to the edge of my panties, hooking his fingers into them and tugging them halfway down my thighs.

He eased his hand between my legs again, his fingers caressing the tender skin of my inner thigh. Sweat broke out on my forehead. I was already throbbing. All I had to do was writhe against his fingers and he'd bring me to an explosive orgasm. Then he leaned forward and stroked his tongue over my clit.

I cried out. Heat boiled through my veins. I fumbled for the doorjamb and held on, trembles wracking my body as he sucked and licked me. It hit me like the strike of a match, a sudden hot flare coursing through my blood.

I came so hard my knees buckled. Cole held me upright until the sensations ebbed and eased away, his eyes dark with satisfaction.

"Your turn," I gasped.

He rose to his feet, bringing one hand to the buttons of his jeans. My mouth watered in anticipation as he flicked the buttons open and pulled his jeans off, leaving him clad in boxer briefs that did nothing to conceal the thick length of his erection.

Arousal and more than a little trepidation flared in me. I cupped my palm against the hard bulge, my whole body softening in readiness.

He pulled me closer and covered my mouth with his again. The earth fell away beneath my feet. I spun downward, endlessly, and the only solid thing in the world was the man holding me against him.

He lowered me onto the bed, pushing his hips between my legs, stroking my breasts. We kissed, touched, and licked, exploring each other's bodies as if we were memorizing every curve and angle.

Cole only moved away from me to retrieve a condom packet from the nightstand. He sheathed his erection and turned back to me, self-restraint lacing his muscles. He slipped his gaze over my naked body, his eyes burning.

"Okay?" he asked.

I nodded, unable to speak past the heat in my throat. He eased my thighs apart and settled between them.

My heart raced, my nerves twisting with longing. I opened my legs wider and dug my fingers into his smooth shoulders. Energy radiated from him, like the sea itself coursed through his veins. He slid partway into me, his movements slow and controlled as he let me adjust to him.

"Cole." I swallowed and forced my body to relax. "Hurry."

I bit down on my lower lip as he pushed farther into me, the invasion both exquisite and intimidating. I arched my hips, encouraging him to thrust even as I braced myself for the pain. He gripped my waist and sank fully inside me, breaching my tender flesh with a power that wrenched a cry from my throat. He swore, his lips coming down hard on mine.

"It's okay," I whispered against his mouth. "I'm okay."

He lifted himself partway off me. Our gazes locked like a chain through the tension-thick air.

"Do it," I gasped, pushing my body upward.

He pulled back and eased forward, not taking his eyes off me, his shoulders tight. Slow at first, a delicious glide stroking me from the inside. Heat unfurled through every part of me. I wrapped my legs around his hips, encouraging him to move faster.

He lowered himself on top of me, bracing his hands on either side of my head, his thrusts shifting to a rhythmic cadence that submerged me in sensation. Sweat dampened his bronzed chest, and his eyes burned.

I never wanted it to end, the rocking and thrusting of our bodies, never wanted to emerge from the haze of lust and need. A sweet, hot urgency expanded inside me, pushing against the barriers of self-restraint.

Sensations burst through my veins, a thousand colors sparking and popping over my skin. I threw my arms around his shoulders as if he were the only secure element in the blissfully spinning whirlwind. His groan echoed against my skin as his body stiffened with his own release. Together, we slowly descended to the other side.

Cole collapsed onto the bed beside me. Our breathing rasped through the hot air. He pulled me to him, tucking me against his side. He threaded a hand through my hair and twisted a few strands around his fingers.

"I love you," I said. The words flew out of my mouth with such ease, as if I'd been storing them in my heart and waiting for the moment when I could open the box and set them free.

He stilled, shock flaring deep in his eyes for an instant before clouding over. My heart constricted.

"Oh, don't," I whispered.

His throat worked with a swallow. "I can't give you anything, Josie. I'm broke as hell and in a shitload of debt. Next summer after I graduate, I'm finally getting out of this town. I don't know what I'm going to do after that...work, grad school, travel, whatever."

"I don't know either." Irritation rippled through me. "And don't use money to try and push me away when this is still about you not thinking you deserve to be loved."

A muscle ticked in his jaw. "You don't want to get stuck with me."

"*Stuck* with you?" I lifted myself onto my elbow. "What are you, Velcro? *I love you, Cole Danforth.* If it's too soon for me to say that, then too damned bad. And no, it's not because we just had sex. I've had a crush on you for a long time, and I know myself well enough to realize that at some point, that crush turned into love.

"I love your strength, your work ethic, your protectiveness, your intelligence. I love that you have a world map on your wall, that you like fart jokes, and that you don't care what people say about you working at the carnival. I love that you open doors for me, stroke my hair, and that sometimes I catch you looking at me with...*awe*, like I'm something miraculous. I love that you brought me my backpack in fourth grade and that you know how a great white shark breathes. But if you can't believe me, then everything I love about you is for *nothing.*"

He stared at me, his eyes dark and his expression implacable, as if he were deflecting every last one of my heartfelt words. My throat tightened to the point of pain.

This was where he was supposed to haul me into his arms and confess how much he loved me too. This was where we kissed, laughed, and realized we'd be deliriously happy living in a shoebox apartment, scraping for rent, and eating canned beans and crackers...because we'd be together and deeply in love.

None of that happened. Cole averted his gaze, his features tensing. Clouds gathered over him again, the approach of a storm.

After pushing the bedcovers aside, I yanked on my clothes. Trembles of anger and hurt rippled through me. Not wanting to give him a chance to say anything—that moment was long past—I shoved my feet into my flip-flops and hurried out the door.

He didn't follow me.

CHAPTER 9

Cole

I'd never liked my birthday. It was a reminder that I was Kevin Danforth's son. Which made it sickeningly ironic that the first thing I did when I turned twenty-three was drive to the Iron Horse Brewery.

Nausea curdled in my gut. I hated the kegs, boilers, conveyers, fermentation tanks. The smells of mashing grain, yeast, sulfur. The noise of the brewpub—mugs hitting the wooden tables, silverware clanging, raucous laughter. Everything about the Iron Horse made me sick.

I walked to my father's office in the back, my muscles tight. He rose from his desk and extended a hand, a pleased expression crossing his face.

"Happy birthday. Glad you could make it."

I stayed by the door and didn't take his hand. I'd wrestled for the past week with whether or not to show up.

The battle had kept my mind off Josie. If I let myself think about her, I'd shatter into a million pieces.

"Sit down." My father gestured to a chair in front of the desk.

"I'll stand."

His jaw tightened, but he gave a casual shrug. "All right. I take it you've read the full letter?"

I nodded. It was a shitload of money set in a *conditional* trust. My father would be the one to determine how much of it I received and when. The thought of giving him that kind of power sparked a firestorm rage in my blood.

But.

If I had the money, I could eradicate my debt. Make a plan for the future. Look into graduate schools without stressing out over tuition and expenses.

I could go to Josie with financial security and—

No.

Having money wouldn't suddenly make me worthy of her. I had no idea what would.

"Your grandfather put this money aside for you to ensure your financial security." My father tapped his finger on a stack of documents. "But he designated me as the trustee because he didn't want you to squander it if you received it in one lump sum. He also wanted to ensure that you were deserving of it. *Worthy.*"

My hands curled into fists. "And?"

"Given the way you've behaved these past few years, you haven't yet proven yourself." He sat down, steepling his fingers. "One of the conditions of the trust, which is not contestable by the way, is that you are to work in a position I designate for at least one year."

Tension gripped my spine. "You want me to work for you."

He held up his hands. "I'm not asking a lot. You can wash kegs, clean the bathrooms, maybe bus tables in the pub. I just want you to exhibit some responsibility and work ethic."

"I work two jobs. I'm a full-time student."

"Maybe." He shrugged. "But how do I know you're telling the truth? You haven't made any attempt to contact me in years."

Anger burned hot in my chest. He wanted me back at the Iron Horse both to control me and so the town residents would think he was such a great father for reconciling with his shitty son.

"And if I don't work for you?"

"You forfeit your right to the money."

Shit. My grandfather, whom I'd never even known, was as manipulative as my father. Controlling us both from the grave.

"Look, I realize we've had a rough relationship." My father ran a hand over his thinning hair. "But you *are* my only son. My only child. I know deep down you're a good kid. I'd like for us to make amends."

How many times had he used this tactic? I knew exactly what he was doing. And I *hated* the dark, buried part of me—so small it was almost invisible—that still wanted to believe him.

"I loved your mother." He stared at his hands, rubbing the finger on which he used to wear his wedding ring. "But she wasn't well. It concerns me terribly that those kinds of disorders are inherited. When you acted out, I was so afraid you were exhibiting the same symptoms as your mother."

I dug my fingernails into my palms. My heart was beating too fast.

"I want you to prove your commitment to me and my company." My father lifted his gaze to mine. "Come and work for me, earn your keep, and we'll get this trust fund sorted out in no time."

I stared at him. The air was hot and suffocating.

"All right?" He lifted his eyebrows in encouragement.

"Fuck you." The words burst out of me like bullets firing.

He blinked. "What did you just say?"

"Fuck. You." I stalked toward the desk, my fists tight enough to break. "You want me to prove my commitment? I don't have a commitment to you or your goddamned company. I hate it here.

I always have. I hate *you*. You're a fucking violent bastard who killed my mother."

He rose to his feet, his mouth compressing and his eyes filling with the dangerous light I knew all too well.

"You watch your mouth, you little shithead," he snapped. "I can see to it that you don't get a dime of this money."

"I don't want a *penny* of it." My tension suddenly dissipated. "Especially not from you."

He rounded the desk and came toward me. Veins throbbed in his forehead, and his face contorted with anger. He brought his hand up—to hit me, grab me, something.

I caught his wrist, blocking the movement. His eyes narrowed. He strained to break free, but I was stronger. I tightened my grip and lowered my head to look him in the eye.

"You are a conman, a liar, and an abuser." After releasing his wrist, I pushed him away. "You know it. I know it. One day this whole town will know it too."

"You're making a big mistake." His eyes blazed. "You're a batshit lunatic to turn down this kind of money. Fucking crazy, just like your mother."

"You can take this *conditional trust...*" I pushed the documents off his desk with one swipe of my arm "...and shove it up your goddamned ass."

I stalked past him to the door, crashing my shoulder against his. He stumbled.

I strode out of the brewpub without looking back. When I reached the parking lot, a sudden lightness filled my chest. Like the sun breaking through a storm.

CHAPTER 10

Josie

"I have a colleague who's doing work with voodoo art." My mother set another bowl of chocolate-chunk ice cream in front of me and patted my shoulder. "I can ask her about ex-boyfriend curses."

I attempted to smile, though if ice cream in the kitchen of my childhood home couldn't make me feel better, voodoo curses certainly wouldn't work.

"No need." Vanessa pulled out the chair across from me, her mouth twisting. "I've got a bunch of ex-boyfriend curses you can borrow."

"I don't want to curse Cole." Glumly, I picked up a spoon and dug into the ice cream. "He's had enough bad stuff in his life. I'm just so bummed he refuses to admit how good we are together."

My mother and sister both clucked in sympathy. In the week since I'd walked out on Cole, I'd been trying to ease my sadness with drawing, ice cream, and a trip up to our Heavenly Daze cabin. Nothing had worked. My sorrow over him and everything we *could have been* was a black-edged shadow surrounding my heart.

"Hey, I have tickets to see *Carousel* in Boston next Saturday," Vanessa said. "My friend Sue has a conflict with a bachelorette party, so I'm sure she won't mind if you use her ticket. We could stay overnight, make a weekend out of it."

I groaned. The word *Carousel* reminded me of riding the Ocean Carousel with Cole, his strong arms caging me in on either side, his thighs hugging my hips, my back pressed to his broad chest.

"I guess that's a no." Vanessa drew her eyebrows together in commiseration.

"I'm sorry." I pushed the bowl away and stood. "Thanks for the offer, but I'd be terrible company."

"Plenty of other men out there," my sister assured me.

"I don't want another man." I picked up my backpack, my heart tightening. "Cole is my chocolate factory."

"My dear daughter." My mother hugged me. "Be your own chocolate factory."

Maybe I could be one day, though that sounded a bit lonely.

After saying goodbye, I headed out into the August sunshine. As I got in the car, my phone buzzed with a text. My heart jumped at the sight of the sender's name.

COLE: Come up to the lighthouse. I want to show you something.

Smothering a surge of hope, I tossed my phone aside and started the car. He'd already blocked my hope and love with a force-field that even the Rebel Alliance couldn't breach. I didn't dare open myself up for hurt again.

I drove over the two-laned road to the Castille Lighthouse, which perched on the top of a rocky cliff overlooking the sea. I parked in the circular lot and hurried up the path to the terrace.

Cole was standing by the old granite wall, known as the "secrets wall" due to the notes scrawled with secrets that people left between the boulders. More than once when I was younger, I'd written *I have a crush on Cole Danforth* on a scrap of paper and pushed it into the rocks. Now, my crush on him was anything but a secret.

A sea wind rumpled his thick brown hair. His blue eyes creased with a cautious smile. My heart began a rhythmic beating, resonant like bells.

I slowed as I approached him, my own wariness sparking to life.

"Hi," he said.

"Hello."

"This is for you." He reached into a paper sack at his feet and brought out a clear plastic bag tied with a bright red ribbon and filled with multiple types of candy.

"What…" I peered at the bag. All my favorites—Lifesavers, gummy bears, Sugar Rush jellies, Starbursts, Jolly Ranchers. All *red.* "Did you pick out all the red ones for me?"

"I sure did. You might even say I *cherry*-picked them." He gave a self-satisfied grin.

I groaned in appreciation. "Thank you. That's so sweet."

"This is also for you." He reached into the bag again and removed the plush raven I'd coveted at the Milk Bottle Toss game booth.

"Aww." I took the stuffed bird, unable to stop a smile from spreading across my face. "How did you get this?"

He frowned, mildly offended. "I won it, fair and square."

"Really?"

"Of course. I had to wait until my shift ended and it took me two tries, but it turns out I have a pretty good pitching arm."

I tucked the bird against my chest. Much as I appreciated the romantic gestures, uncertainty still simmered in my blood. I'd put all my emotions on the line for him and gotten unyielding, hard silence in return. A bag of red candies and a plush bird couldn't make my lingering pain go away.

"So, I had this big plan to put a secret in the wall and tell you to find it." Cole stepped toward me, his expression sobering. "But then I realized that would be stupid since I don't want this to be a secret anymore."

Butterflies danced in my stomach. "You don't want what to be a secret?"

"My love for you."

My heart leapt with a surge of joy so strong it resonated through every part of me. "Oh."

"Hold on." He took the candy and bird from me and set them on the wall so he could wrap his big hands around mine. "I have a whole speech for you."

He took a breath, faint nervousness rising to his eyes. "You were right when you said I had a crush on you when we were kids, but I never believed we'd ever really find our way to each other. And when we did...well, when you threw yourself at me with wild abandon..."

I chuckled, heat rising to my cheeks. He cupped my face in his hand. Tender warmth filled his eyes.

"I've never considered myself lucky," he said. "Not with my childhood or anything else really. But the instant you kissed me, I felt like the luckiest man in the world. And when you actually came looking for me...it was like I'd won the lottery. I couldn't believe it was happening. That Josie Mays wanted to be with me. And someday I'll have more to offer you, but right now all I can tell you is that I love you so damned much.

"I give you my heart, my body to do with as you please, and my promise that I'll always protect you. I love your courage, your strength, the way you squint when you're drawing, your nerdy knowledge about birds, and the fact that you didn't let go of my hand when we leapt off the cliff."

Tears filled my eyes. "You didn't let go of me either."

"I never will." He tightened his fingers on mine, his mouth curving with the beautiful smile that never failed to warm me right down to my soul. "I love you, Josie."

"I love you, Cole. I have loved you for a very long time."

He slipped his hand under my chin, lifting my face to his. Our lips met in a warm, lovely kiss that made my entire being glow with light. Tears slipped down my cheeks. He eased back, brushing my tears away with his thumbs before digging into the pocket of his jeans.

"Triple ply." He proudly held up a thick white tissue. "With lotion, aloe, and vitamin E."

With a laugh, I took the tissue and wiped my eyes.

"Cole Danforth, you really are my hero."

It was our *happy ever before*.

For the next year, we wrapped ourselves around each other like a ball of yarn. We were tender and volatile. We argued about miscommunication, my absent-mindedness, his tendency to make plans without asking me first. We laughed until we cried. We went hiking and swimming. We played checkers and studied for classes. We had wild, fulfilling sex. *A lot.* We moved in together, scrimped, saved, and planned for the future.

Cole Danforth was my first crush, my first lover, my *only* love. In my girlhood days when I'd dreamed about a lifelong love, he'd been the one who always came to mind. The one I wished for. And in my twentieth year, I lived with a translucent, shimmering wish come true.

Then the wish ruptured, exploding from the inside, firing

shards of metal straight through my heart. From the burnt ashes, a new wish formed, misshapen and ugly.

I wish I'd never known Cole Danforth.

Thank you for reading IF WE LEAP!

Josie and Cole's story continues in IF WE FALL and IF WE FLY.

ABOUT THE AUTHOR

New York Times & USA Today bestselling author Nina Lane writes hot, sexy romances about professors, bad boys, candy makers, and protective alpha males who find themselves consumed with love for one woman alone. Originally from California, Nina holds a PhD in Art History and an MA in Library and Information Studies, which means she loves both research and organization. She also enjoys traveling and thinks St. Petersburg, Russia is a city everyone should visit at least once. Although Nina would go back to college for another degree because she's that much of a bookworm and a perpetual student, she now lives the happy life of a full-time writer.

www.ninalane.com

ALSO BY NINA LANE

THE SECRET THIEF

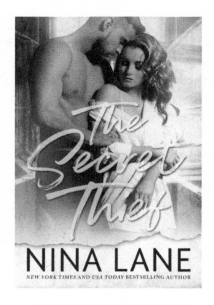

"This book is a work of art."

Escaping the disgrace of a scandal, art historian Eve Perrin runs away to the coastal town of Castille, Maine, where she encounters a mysterious lighthouse keeper who has dark secrets of his own.

THE SUGAR RUSH SERIES

Taste the sweetness of life.

From the Stone family patriarch down to the youngest bad boy, follow the lives and loves of the Sugar Rush men in Nina's sexy, compelling series.

THE SPIRAL OF BLISS SERIES

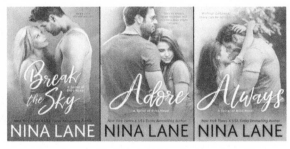

"Give me a kiss, beauty."

From an exhilarating crush to the intensities of marriage, Liv and Dean West embark on a passionate lifelong journey together. As the medieval history professor and his beloved wife face both personal challenges and painful battles, they never lose sight of the hope, humor, and devotion that belong only to them.

Liv and Dean's everlasting romance will melt your heart, turn you on, and enchant you with the power of a love to end all loves.

Made in United States
North Haven, CT
04 February 2023

32057638R00061